PRAISE FOR WES RAND

"The unconventional collected works of Wes Rand was recommended to me. I can say these are not for the whimsical as you'll wish that only bandits, outlaws, and wildlife, are the only things to fear. Bring a gun as you sit down to read and pray you are not on the wrong side of Major Neville Stryker."

— **DIANE KAWASAKI**, WRITER AND STAR OF TLC'S HIT SHOW MY LITTLE LIFE

"Gritty, dark, and fast-paced—If you love frontier action, Wes Rand's EVIL STRYKER SERIES will knock you out of the saddle."

— *ERIC J. GUIGNARD*, AWARD-WINNING AUTHOR, AND EDITOR, INCLUDING *AFTER DEATH…* AND *BAGGAGE OF ETERNAL NIGHT*, BRAM STOKER AWARD-WINNER

"As a filmmaker, I can see the vibrant images come to life on every page as Evil Stryker crosses every line of decency and yet leaves the women wanting him and the men wanting to be him. Wes has created an anti-hero of devastating impact."

— **VINCENT ROCCA**, WRITER/DIRECTOR OF *KISSES AND CAROMS*, AUTHOR OF *11 SIMPLE STEPS TO TURN A SCREENPLAY INTO A MARKETABLE MOVIE: OR, HOW I GOT A $10K MOVIE TO GROSS $1 MILLION THROUGH WARNER BROS*

"A wild ride through the old west, filled with unforgettable characters and plenty of action. This series hits all the marks! You're going to love Evil Stryker!"

— **JOHN PALISANO,** VICE PRESIDENT OF THE
HORROR WRITERS ASSOCIATION AND BRAM
STOKER AWARD-WINNING AUTHOR OF *NIGHT OF
1,000 BEASTS*

"Evil Stryker operates like a confident, skilled executioner across its violent Western landscape."

— **DALLAS SONNIER**, PRODUCER OF BONE
TOMAHAWK

UNDERCOVER WORK

UNDERCOVER WORK

Book VIII of the Evil Stryker Series

WES RAND

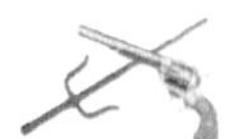

UNDERCOVER WORK

BOOK VIII IN THE EVIL STRYKER SERIES

Copyright © 2024 by Wes Rand

Cover Copyright © 2024 by Wes Rand

Published by Wild West Books

All Rights Reserved.

Cover Illustration by Linda Nilsen Worker
lindanilsenworker.com

Editing Services and Formatting: Stacey Smekofske EditsByStacey.com

Printed in the United States of America.

ISBN Paperback: 979-8-9883083-2-4

ISBN ePub: 979-8-9883083-3-1

For my Family

CHAPTER ONE

It was a bright sunny day in Berkeley, one of three for the month. Two large rectangular, four-story buildings built in Napoleon III style, North and South Hall, stood on a hill overlooking the young California town. The campus lay in a clearing surrounded by a forest of coastal live oak, broadleaf maple, California laurel, willows, and a variety of native shrubs. The adjacent area was mostly farms established in the 1880s. North and South Halls were the first two buildings on the new College of California campus. Other structures like the science, medical, library, laboratory, cafeteria, and dormitory buildings were in the planning stages. The College of California in Berkeley opened in 1855. In 1868, it was renamed the University of California.

It was noon on the grounds in front of South Hall, when a crowd of sixty people sat on folding chairs, eagerly waiting for the speaker. The wooden lectern waited, unoccupied. Behind the lectern, a four-story brick building was dressed in a navy-blue banner that stretched above the double-door entrance. "University of California" was sewn in gold lettering on the banner. Collis Huntington, one of *The Big Four* railroad men was credited with building northern California, (the other three being Leland Stanford, Charles Crocker, and Mark Hopkins). Huntington was to be the guest speaker. Collis, a crafty persuader, wore a heavy beard to make up for the dearth of hair on his head. The University President, Edward Holden, sat in the front row. President Holden, a self-made man, and a former member of the United States House of Representatives, sported a full beard beneath his piercing gray eyes. To his left, Phoebe Hearst sat patiently. She was a stout and purposeful woman, and she was the wife of Senator George Hearst. Collis sat on the other side of Mrs. Hearst.

The Governor, Robert Waterman, would have made it to the gathering but had taken ill and begged off from attending his good friend's speech. Plenty of other dignitaries were in the front rows anyway. Stanford, Crocker, Hopkins, and other prominent business leaders took up the rest of the front row. Slightly less prominent attendees sat in the second row. In the third and fourth rows other businessmen, local officials, college deans, professors, and a smattering of individuals sought to rub elbows with the higher-ups.

A person seated by herself in the third row should also be recognized. She was a mining engineer for Senator George Hearst. An attractive widow in her mid-thirties, her husband had been murdered. She and her husband had owned a ranch and mine which had been stolen from them by a gang of thuggish politicos. With help from an unlikely source, she regained the properties and sold them. Shortly afterward, Hearst persuaded her to work for him. Her name is Morgan Bickford. Some thought her good looks helped get the job. That probably didn't hurt. Miss Bickford was an excellent geologist, but she was more than that to the senator. Not sexually, Hearst was too old to sample her charms. Exchanging kisses on cheeks and warm embraces were enough to show reciprocal fondness. Senator Hearst sent Morgan to represent him since he was in Washington D.C.

Students sat in the back half of the audience. Males made up three-quarters of the students, females the remaining quarter, and they were seated separately. Women attending college had yet to be fully embraced.

A steady hum rose from mundane conversations in the audience. Nothing note-worthy, just idle chatter about the weather, mutual acquaintances, or other routine topics.

At a quarter past twelve, President Holden turned to the crowd behind him, satisfied the chairs looked largely occupied, he rose and approached the speaker's podium. Chatter faded, except for two people conversing in the rear. Suddenly realizing everyone could hear them, they abruptly stopped talking. The President smiled and nodded at guests important enough to recognize, and then he cleared his throat to speak.

"Today on this special occasion, we gather to dedicate the newly completed agriculture building, named in honor of our very generous benefactor who has been so instrumental in the establishment of California's first university. First, Mister Collis Huntington, would like to say a few words. Mister Huntington." President Holden extended his hand in the direction of Collis, then led the applause.

Collis rose to his feet, walked to the podium, and shook hands with President Holden. The President then took Huntington's seat next to Mrs. Hearst.

"Thank you, President Holden," Collis began. "Ladies and gentlemen, Mrs. Hearst, honored guests, faculty and students, and local members of our community, I would like to thank you for joining us on this fine auspicious day for the dedication of the new University of California Agriculture Building. This is also to commemorate the eleventh year of the Mining and Mechanical Arts Building." Huntington nodded at Phoebe Hearst and started a round of applause for her. Collis continued his speech which mentioned California's important history in mining and the University's part in it. He also talked about the importance of the railroads, and how his involvement aided in the economic boon to California. His speech was planned for a full forty-five boring minutes. It only lasted ten.

A booming drumbeat sounded through the trees, a distant steady ominous thumping from a bass drum. A group of around thirty young men and women emerged, carrying signs and chanting. Marching in step with the drumbeat they advanced toward the seated attendees. The protestors wore black handkerchiefs to mask their faces, leaving only their eyes visible.

The mob marched closer. The chants grew louder and more angry. "FROM EACH ACCORDING TO HIS ABILTY, TO EACH

ACCORDING TO HIS NEED!" They chanted with raised fists, shaking them in cadence.

"What is this?" Huntington asked. He turned from the approaching mob to look at President Holden who glared at the protesters.

Many of the guests looked puzzled. Some asked, "Is this part of a performance?" Or words to that effect.

Protesters marched around seated guests, repeating the same mantra, shaking their fists, and brandishing signs. The signs said things like, "Proletarians of the World, Unite! Capitalism Enriches the Few, Enslaves the Many! Workers Unite! Power to the People!"

Marchers crowded closer to guests, taunting them. Some of the male students pushed back; however, other students joined in and the protest erupted into a brawl. That is when marchers pulled hidden batons and used the weapons to club people.

President Holden jumped to his feet, yelling for the fighting to stop, but he was ignored.

Holden ordered dignitaries to follow him into the new agriculture building. As a West Point graduate, Edward Holden knew where to take a defensive stance. Mrs. Hearst, Huntington, Morgan, and others ran after Holden for the building. They burst through the heavy oak doors and took refuge in the foyer. At the foyer's other end, swing doors led to the classroom corridor. Holden locked the front doors, leaving the swing doors available for escape if needed. Steel-framed casement windows on each side of the front doors provided both security and light for the refugees. The escapees cloistered in the entrance area, subdued and quiet, shocked into silence by the violent eruptions outside.

Holden broke from the group and rushed to a window for a view of the melee outside. Morgan moved behind him to watch as well.

"Damn! Look at those two, Woolsey and Palusi. What the hell are they doing?" Holden pointed at two women standing in the third row of chairs, laughing, and clapping their hands in rhythm with the drumbeat. Half the protesters marched and chanted, while the rest clubbed defenseless students. The front two rows of seats were empty with overturned chairs. Woolsey and Palusi, two adjunct professors in the political science department, joined the protesters and marched with them.

Hollis and Mrs. Hearst remained a few feet away from the group quietly discussing cutting off future donations to the university.

"These people don't look like regular students," Holden fumed. "They're too organized. Who the hell are they?"

A male student with a bloody face staggered toward the building. He fell and lay on the ground unmoving.

"I'd like to find out who's behind these damn bastard . . ." Holden's spit splattered the glass. He frustratingly banged his fist on the wall.

"Assholes," Morgan supplied

Holden turned, surprised by the frank description from her.

"Yes, I said assholes," she reiterated.

"I would really like to know who's behind this mob." Holden swung back to the window.

"I know a man who can probably find out," Morgan offered.

Holden faced her again. "You know such a man?" he asked, arching his eyebrows.

"Yes."

"He might have to be undercover, it's a dangerous duty. What's his name?"

"Stryker."

Two miles west of the tiny Northern California town of Pescadero, a pair of steely gray eyes watched ocean waves roll in and crash on a sandy beach. The beach was down the twenty-foot escarpment from the man who sat on his horse. Some folks say Neville Stryker was a ruthless killer.

Standing, he rose to six feet three inches, and tipped the scales at two hundred pounds, give or take a beer or two. His angular unfriendly facial features placed his age in the late thirties. His weathered face showed crow's feet radiating from piercing pale eyes. His intense eyes resembled those of a predator bird; the fine lines radiating from them were not laugh lines. His black hair, graced by a few white ones these days, hung straight to the shoulders. A week-old beard ran along his jawline. He wore his mustache Mexican style, drooping at the ends. The denim shirt and jeans were recently washed but were well-worn. The black Stetson on his crown was likewise well-used, dusty from years on the trail.

A .44-40 Winchester rested in the saddle boot. He carried a .44 Colt Peacemaker in his gun belt, the same ammunition in both guns. A razor in the rear pocket was for shaving—most of the time— but the weapon strapped in the small of his back chilled men's spines. The sai was a steel fork-like weapon with three prongs, the center tine being the longest. The sai was once an Asian farming tool modified to use against the sword. Normally used in pairs, Stryker carried only one. It worked for him. Stryker had sometimes used it to kill those who crossed him. Most enemies occupied graves. Stryker's foes didn't convalesce, they decomposed.

Brought up by his Asian uncle in San Francisco, a master of tai kung fu, Stryker learned how to defend himself, becoming proficient with the sai in his teens. Two older boys, sons of the union thugs who had killed his parents on the Embarcadero, made his life even more miserable by regularly beating the hell out of him. That was until he turned fourteen and killed them. He got each boy on the ground in a dark alley and rammed the sai down their throats. After that, his uncle sent him east. The move probably saved his life. While there he got caught up in the Civil War.

Stryker was at one time a major in the United States Army, and he was once married. He had been out of the army for several years now, and his wife was long dead. She died during an artillery firepower demonstration gone wrong. Most of the blame for her death was due to a weapons company competitor switching target coordinates. Stryker had rammed a saber through the man's gut. Since then, he had been wanted for the murder. President Cleveland had offered him a presidential pardon, but for reasons known only to himself, he refused it. The rest of the blame for his wife's death rested on *his* shoulders. He should have checked the howitzer settings. He hadn't. Since then, nightmares about Leigh, the dead wife, have plagued his nights. Most of them were about finding her bloodied and dying. She died in his arms with his name on her lips.

His lineage was Mexican, Asian, and Scandinavian—a mixed breed. He didn't know much about his heritage and hadn't cared enough to learn. His parents were killed when he was age seven, and he can't remember much of what they told him about his ancestors.

Today he sat astride a roan horse, watching the sea on a much-traveled saddle that once had the name "MAJOR NEVILLE STRYKER" stenciled on the saddle skirt. Usage and weather wore off a few letters. Most people say what's left is more fitting, "EVIL STRYKER."

Stryker spends time resting between jobs in Pescadero. The jobs are for Senator George Hearst. Hearst made his fortune working the Comstock Lode in Virginia City. He won the *San Francisco Examiner* newspaper in a poker game and had trouble collecting on the bet. Hearst desperately wanted the paper for his son, William Randolf Hearst. Morgan Bickford recommended Stryker to help with the transfer. Stryker succeeded in getting the deed signed over to Hearst, and the senator paid Stryker one hundred thousand dollars. The recalcitrant owner of the newspaper had not survived the transaction.

Morgan's help with regaining her ranch and mine before working for Hearst was from Stryker's involvement. He *was* the unlikely source. The two had struck a deal. He would receive half proceeds from the property sale–if he got it returned to her. He did, and she paid him.

Stryker had no real friends, but he did jobs for the senator and sometimes sampled the charms of Morgan. He usually stayed away from the woman, only visiting her occasionally. Since his wife's death, whenever he got involved with another woman, she ended up dead. A jinx. At one time, he thought Morgan had been killed too; however, she survived the gunshot wound, and Stryker kept his distance from her, thinking the curse might allow her to live. The jinx is the main reason Stryker spent time between jobs in Pescadero. Stryker was not a man given to the metaphysical, but he believed this maddening, lethal curse wouldn't leave him alone. Horrific nightmares of his dead wife wouldn't leave him alone either. The man was deadly proficient with the .44 Colt, sai, and razor, but he could not kill the nightmares.

Secret missions for Hearst gave Stryker something to do with his life. Stryker was not a man to remain idle for long. Hearst paid him well. Also, the senator had once saved his life when Stryker worked in the Big Basin near Felton where the giant redwoods grow. Hearst sent a U.S. Army unit to prevent lumberjacks from chopping Stryker to death for killing one of their own. Stryker later found out Morgan had a hand in saving him. The senator had saved his life, and Stryker sustained the obligation. He owed Morgan, too. He's killed for her.

Stryker swung the roan south along the meandering trail above the escarpment, causally watching waves break on the beach below. The early morning fog lifted, burned off by the sun, and the day began with a clear sky. Sea lions barked on sea stacks reaching up between blankets of floating kelp. Honking seagulls circled lazily and then raced along the tops of waves looking for breakfast. Sandpipers ran across the sand searching for small crustaceans washed up by waves. Wafts of briny saltwater enhanced the visual of sea life activity. There was no other smell like that of the ocean. A mile or so later he came to the piece of driftwood he pulled up earlier from the beach, and he used it as a bench. The mixed breed sometimes sat and watched ships sail up and down the coast. Today he reined in the roan and dismounted, letting the reins hang loose. The roan never wandered far; there were plentiful white clover and ice plants to munch nearby. Stryker wiped off the bench and sat.

Stryker was not prone to long periods of reflection; however, he did take extended periods in Pescadero for rest and recreation. "R and R," they called it in the military. The times away from the quiet little town were not usually relaxing.

It had been a few months, and his time in Pescadero had become boring. He thought about Morgan. He wouldn't mind seeing her. She felt good under him. He liked the way she moved enjoying herself. As good as the sex was, it was the woman's mind he liked more. Morgan thought in a straight line, no idle ruminations, no jokes, and no fact rounding. Being a principled, disciplined woman was her only indulgence. Self-indulgence was with the man who sat on the bench. He never questioned why she indulged him. It was not a good idea to inspect a gift horse too closely, but he did theorize about highly intelligent women he had known (in the biblical sense). They often led intense, studious lives, long tiresome work, and when they let their hair down, it fell all the way down. Intelligent girls were the best. They were willing to experiment, and Morgan was a very bright girl. Stryker found brainy girls were not self-conscious. Although, they do request, or demand, to be pleasured. When a woman like that lets loose, she really needed her itch scratched, and apparently, Morgan liked how Stryker scratches.

Once Senator Hearst asked Morgan why she liked Stryker. Maybe he said "liked" rather than "slept with" to be polite. Regardless, Morgan responded with, "He rings with good steel. I trust him with my life, and he's killed for me."

On that morning, Stryker sat on the bench and looked out over the emerald sea thinking about scratching Morgan's itch.

After a few more minutes, Stryker rose, gathered the horse reins, and swung onto the saddle. The roan, sensing it was headed back to oats in the stable, quickened its pace. Stryker rested his hand on the saddle horn, loosely holding the reins, The big horse didn't need directions. The trail to town ran along the Pescadero Marsh, a fresh water wetland with dense riparian woods and coastal scrub. Herons, egrets, and nearly 200 additional bird species lived and nested in the marsh. Stryker took it in before crossing Butano Creek and returning to Pescadero. He'd had a restful, albeit bordering on boring, morning.

Elena was in her late forties and owned the boarding house where Stryker rented a room. She had steak and eggs waiting for him. How she knew when he would return from his morning ride, he hadn't figured out. He'd ask her sometime. Elena was part Mexican, part European herself —a mixed breed like Stryker. They got along well. The steak and eggs were warm and the coffee was black, strong, and hot.

The *San Francisco Examiner* lay beside his plate. Stryker knew Elena wasn't particularly happy about providing him with the paper because Morgan placed Hearst's job requests in the personals section. The ads likely meant he would leave soon, usually for a long period of time. He wondered why Elena disliked the absences. Was it the money, or another reason, maybe one more personal? If he asked, she would probably say, money, and keep the real reason to herself. The other newspapers Elena gave him were several days old. While he ate, he casually turned the pages until he got to the personals section. Scrolling through the postings with his forefinger, he searched for a listing from Morgan. Finding them was good, and not so good, news for Stryker. Good news because it meant Morgan still lived and he would soon see her. Then again, maybe it would not be good if Hearst had another dangerous mission.

Stryker found a post for him this morning.

MORGAN'S BEEN KIDNAPPED

CHAPTER TWO

Normally, the trip to San Francisco took the better part of two days. The ride from Pescadero over the Santa Cruz Mountains to Saratoga was a day-and-a-half ride by horseback, with stops in a rest shack on the mountain or the Congress Springs Hotel in Saratoga. No rail service connected Pescadero to San Francisco directly. At Saratoga, a spur line ran to San Jose, and from there the Southern Pacific Railroad took passengers to San Francisco. Stryker rested the roan and himself in a trail cabin for a few hours during the night. Then he started out before dawn the next day. There was no stopping at the Congress Springs Hotel on this trip.

Maybe it was the jinx. Maybe not. Either way, Stryker couldn't sit in Pescadero and wait for news on Morgan. He caught the spur train in Saratoga and then boarded the Southern Pacific in San Jose. No use speculating about the abduction. He would get more information from Hearst. The old man, using resources afforded to a U.S. Senator, would have all available intelligence on the kidnapping. One thing Stryker figured was someone in the shadows knew about it. He was not a man who used torture to make a person talk. It was not his style. Kill a man yes, but not torture. He would have Hearst send for Tooonug. The Paiute Indian and Stryker had dealings in the past when he had trouble in Tahoe[i]. The unlikely partnership worked before. During which, Stryker learned how effectively Tooonug could get information from a reluctant informant. All the informants eventually talked, and none survived the conversations.

Hours rolled on slowly for Stryker, slower than the Shay locomotive that only had a maximum speed of twenty miles an hour. Narrow gauge rails wouldn't allow for a more rapid speed even if the coal-fired engine could travel faster. Stryker read more up-to-date editions of the *Examiner* and stared out the window to pass the time. It was not necessary to return greetings. There were none. His fearsome features did not invite conversation. Stryker made it a habit to sit in the rear seat. Most riders chose benches nearer the front and away from the menacing-looking man.

The train rolled into San Francisco's Ferry House at 2:15 p.m. After stabling the roan with the station hostler, Stryker stepped aboard the Market Street cable car to the Palace Hotel.

The Palace Hotel was widely regarded as the finest hotel in the world when it opened in 1875. Each of the 755 rooms had a fireplace and a private bathroom with toilet and tub. Above the Grand Court's carriage entrance and turn around, seven floors, rectangular shaped, and with ornate white columns paced every few feet on the overlooking balconies. Each guest room had a large bay window to enjoy the views of the city or the bay. The Palace had its own oak forest from which trees were harvested. That is not to say oak was the only wood found in the grand hotel. There was dark mahogany or redwood paneling in dining rooms, on banister railings, and the six-foot high front desk. Giant pots of magnificent ferns sat throughout the first floor. The lobby on the ground level, a cavernous twenty-five feet in height awed arriving guests. Redwood paneled and hydraulically operated rising rooms were among the first elevators in the world to swoop lodgers to upper floors. The spacious men's and women's dining rooms had tables covered with silk linens. The bar with etched glass, marble, and polished brass figurines on the corners was without equal in the world and served only the finest libations. Numerous hotel attachés catered to every whim or need. Business magnets and high-ranking politicians, including presidents, gathered at the Palace Hotel to discuss business and politics. Being seen at the Palace was a big deal. People dressed their best and conducted themselves with the utmost propriety. Of course, Stryker marched in with worn denim, dusty boots, and a .44 on his hip, which fit right in. He entered through the grand buggy entrance located on New Montgomery Street.

Stryker skirted by the buggies parked in the bricked roundabout court walked past the seven-foot potted ferns bracketing the arched entryway to the hotel, and entered the lobby. He crossed the marble floor to the massive check-in counter. The mahogany desk, although meant to impress with its size, was thirty feet wide and seven feet tall, but it seemed much too imposing to be a friendly welcome for guests. It was impressive but imposing. A lower open window in the center allowed space for eight to ten people to register at the same time, depending on their girths.

A desk clerk, in a uniformed maroon jacket with tails, tan red-striped trousers, a maroon bowtie, and a starched white shirt saw Stryker approaching. He waved him to an open space at the desk.

"Mister Stryker, welcome. One moment while I call the senator." The smartly dressed clerk greeted him with a broad smile. A freshly scrubbed young man in his mid-twenties knew the drill. Extend the utmost courtesies to the tall, stern-looking man. Those were Senator Hearst's instructions. Stryker was not a man to rile. The clerk turned, leaned over the speaking tube, and pressed a button. "Mister Stryker for you, sir." He put his ear near the tube and nodded. "Will do, sir."

"The Senator says to come right up."

Stryker started to walk away from the desk when the clerk called out to him, "And sir, here is your key to *810*." Room *810* was for Stryker's use. Hearst always arranged for him to have a room at the Palace Hotel while visiting San Francisco. It was on the same floor as the Senator's. Hearst's room was at the end of the hallway and had a better view of the city and bay.

Stryker took the key, shoved it in his shirt pocket, and headed for the rising room around the corner. When he rounded the corner, a small crowd of people, mostly men, waiting for the hydraulic elevator. The car arrived and the crowd parted to let those in the elevator empty out. Stryker muscled his way closer to the doorway.

"Just a moment, sir." The elevator operator raised his hand to stop Stryker from entering the car. Then he said, "Sorry, sir. Please step in." The other guests waiting did not object. They must have figured Stryker to be a very important person, or maybe they figured the Colt Peacemaker on his hip was enough to provide special privileges. Everyone except two middle-aged women decided to wait for the next car. Why the men waited is anybody's guess. Could have been they thought trouble just stepped inside the elevator and wanted no part of it. The two women entered behind Stryker.

"What floor, ladies?" The operator asked as he closed the brass gate.

"Five please," the women answered at the same time. They paid no attention to Stryker. Staring straight ahead at the passing floors, they said nothing and got off when the elevator reached the fifth floor.

The women reminded Stryker of a few he'd known in the past. Women are stronger than men when faced with danger or adversity. He'd marveled at their fortitude at the time. Some had been brutally tortured and withstood it. Then he thought about Morgan. *Where the hell is she?* The elevator came to a stop.

"Eighth floor, sir," the operator announced, opening the gate.

Stryker stepped onto emerald green carpeting and walked down the hall in long purposeful strides. The senator's gold-framed door hung open, and he heard men talking from inside the room. Stryker entered without knocking.

"Stryker!" Hearst saw him first. "Come in. We were just talking about Morgan." Senator George Hearst, in his late sixties, stood a rail-thin thin six feet in height, sported a long gray beard, and had cold hard eyes that could drill through a man. He and Stryker got along well.

"Stryker, this is Chief of Police, Brock. He was just telling me about some clues regarding Morgan's disappearance." Hearst took Brock's arm and guided him to greet Stryker, clueing Stryker on how things stacked up between the two men.

"Call me, Cameron." Chief Brock extended his hand, but Stryker ignored it. In a move meant to look less awkward, Brock swept his hand upward and tugged on an earlobe. Cameron stood a portly five feet, six inches. He wasn't obese. However, the buttons struggled mightily on the front of his navy blue uniform. Between the thinning red hair and the full beard, Brock's ruddy face suggested he might down a few daily beers. However, his eyes appeared sharp and intelligent beneath the bushy eyebrows. Okay, he looked the part of a well-fed, veteran policeman.

The two-room suite was luxurious but in a masculine way with lots of Honduran mahogany paneling. Chairs around the conference table were also made from mahogany as well as the lathed wood on two maroon wingback chairs. The wingbacks by the bay window afforded views of sailing ships in the San Francisco Bay. An oak chest with brass hardware sat between the chairs. A glass tray holding a bottle of Grand Marnier cognac and two brandy glasses sat on the chest. Hearst had a learned taste for the orange-flavored spirit. The huge conference table was built from dark teak wood, and inlaid glass with an etched redwood covered the tabletop. An overstuffed, maroon settee sat along the wall opposite the bay window. Across from the entrance door, there was a second room with a bed, desk, chair, and toilet.

"Cameron told me four nights ago witnesses saw Morgan having dinner with three men in the Tadich Grill on California Street," Hearst said. "That was the last time she was seen. She didn't show up the next morning."

"We think it was her," Brock added. "A man and woman who claim to know Miss Bickford were having dinner in the restaurant and sat nearby."

"Did they hear the discussion?" Stryker asked.

"Well, yes they did," Brock said. "Said it was talk about mining and problems with it, pumping water out of the mines, that sort of thing. They heard the name Starr used a couple of times."

"I want to talk with that couple," Stryker said.

"Might take a while." Brock didn't seem too pleased with Stryker's demand. "They took the ferry to Alameda yesterday." A sarcastic smile wormed its way onto his face.

"Can you give us their names and when they'll be back?" Hearst asked quickly, thinking Stryker might punch the chief.

"Fred and Estelle, Leonard." Brock answered somewhat cautiously, eying Stryker.

"And when they might return, Cameron?" Hearst sought to maintain civility. After all, he and the chief were good friends, and Brock had helped the senator with a few sensitive situations that only a well-informed police chief could handle.

Brock turned to Hearst. "Gone across the bay to visit a sister. Ramona's her name, I think. Be gone a few days, I think. Not sure. Just a guess." Hearst had aided the chief a few times as well.

"Shit," cursed Stryker.

"Any other information, Cameron? Anything at all?" Hearst asked. "You know I'm very fond of Morgan." Affections shared between the senator and Morgan had their limitations, but nevertheless, he wanted Brock to understand that this was a special case, a very special case.

"I'm afraid I don't have much else to add, George. I can get the sister's address if you like."

"How soon?" Stryker asked with less acid. He needed Brock's help.

"Maybe later today. I'll get out a telegram right away." Brock directed his response more to Hearst than Stryker. "I'm not sure if Ramona's last name is Leonard. She could be married." The policeman picked up his hat. "I'll do my best, George." With that, Brock turned and walked from the room.

"Stryker, I think you should pay Estelle's sister a visit when Cameron gets her address." Hearst stepped to the chest. "Wanna a drink?" He asked as he poured two fingers of cognac into a glass.

"No."

Hearst took a long sip of cognac. "Dammit." He took another to finish it and set the glass on the tray. "Don't like it. Don't like it at all."

Stryker knew the senator was not talking about the cognac.

Hearst spun away from the window. "You've got to find her, Stryker." The old man sounded plaintive. "And Stryker, you know I only have a fatherly interest in Morgan. Shouldn't be wanting another wife, anyway. But hell, dammit, if I lost Phoebe, I'd probably go out and find another woman I couldn't stand and buy her a house, too."

Stryker nodded. He stepped to the window and looked out over the city and the bay beyond. Morgan Bickford brought a sense of permanence to his life. A connection to a life he had not known in a long time. Although Morgan provided notices in the *Examiner* for secretive missions, she did represent some semblance of a normal life for him. Between Leigh's death and meeting her, his life had been a relentless run of violent encounters, some of it his own making. To be honest, almost all was his own making. Stryker is not an easy man to be around. Even with Morgan, the first interaction was bloody. Some of it was Morgan's. Stryker thought she'd been killed and he left town in the middle of the night. The town was called Egalitaria, formally named Bickford after Morgan and her husband. Her husband was murdered several months before Stryker rode into Egalitaria. The widow hired him to retrieve the ranch and mine illegally taken from her by Marxist thugs. Stryker secured the ranch and mine for Morgan, but during the gunfire, she was critically wounded. Her teenage son, who despised Stryker, told him Morgan was dead. Stryker didn't know very much about Morgan back then. However, he did like and admire the woman, and her supposed death hit him hard. Another tragic loss due to the jinx plaguing him; anyone who got close, died. It didn't make sense, of course, but the deaths kept happening.

Several months later, he learned she had survived the gunshot.

Stryker would only have one wife, Leigh. He and Morgan would never marry. She knew that and was fine with it. A second marriage for her wasn't in the cards either. It was not because of devotion to her deceased husband, though. Her husband was now dead, and Stryker was her man. Morgan understood that for reasons known only to Stryker, whether it was devotion to his dead wife, or because he told her women close to him don't live long, or for some other unknown reason, he would never ask for her hand in marriage. They had an accord, affections unsaid. One other thing endeared her to Stryker, Morgan never met a man like him, a man who would, and has in the past . . . killed for her.

As for the mixed breed, Morgan was an intelligent woman, attractive in many ways, not just with physical beauty, but more importantly her principles and moral values; *a man (or woman) has the right to live for one's purpose.* Stryker respected and admired Morgan, and she had a warm bed for him when he rode into town.

Stryker was not a man given to flowery words of affection. A no-bullshit man, he never used the word *love* with Leigh, Morgan, or any woman. Women knew how he felt. He wasn't much of a dancer either. Those moves he said, were better used between the sheets.

He turned from the window. Hearst was pouring himself another cognac.

"What do you think, Stryker? Can you bring her home?" The glass in the senator's hand was shaking.

"First, I have to find out who to kill."

Hearst had heard the rumors. Adversaries encountered on the senator's missions did not fare well. If death had eyes, they would look like Stryker's, and the pale ghostly eyes told the senator, Stryker meant what he said.

Hearst nodded, and Stryker headed for the door.

"Stryker," Hearst called out. "What you gonna do now?"

"Tadich Grill." Stryker flung open the door and started down the hall.

Outside the room, Stryker walked to the rising room and tried to think of questions to ask restaurant personnel. *Who waited on Morgan's table? Who was with her at the table? Names? Did they look friendly? Did they leave together?* He also wanted to see where she sat. He was no detective. He knew that. The restaurant people had probably been questioned by the police, but maybe they had missed something. Besides, going there was better than sitting on his ass. The two middle-aged couples stopped talking when Stryker got on the elevator. They made room for him by crowding near the rear. Stryker ignored them and the seven more guests who boarded the elevator on lower floors. They gave him plenty of room. No one spoke until Stryker stepped into the lobby, and then he heard whispered comments behind him about his rudeness and rugged attire. On a different night, he might have turned and told them to get back on the elevator.

He walked from the hotel and onto Market Street. There he hopped on the cable car and rode it to Battery Street. His cowboy boots weren't conducive to streets paved with cobblestones, and of course, it was drizzling rain. The damp chill and a strong breeze numbed his hands. He stuffed them in his pockets. He could have hailed a horse cab after leaving the cable car, but he wasn't in the mood. Instead, he walked the remaining two blocks to the grill on California Street.

A little after six in the evening, the restaurant wasn't very crowded. Stryker walked in and he saw four empty seats at the horseshoe bar and two vacant booths along the wall. The kitchen sat in the rear where four cooks busily prepared meals behind the chest-high counter. The head chef barked orders to the other three. Grilling smoke billowed up and over the counter greeting customers with an enticing aroma. The Tadich Grill, a popular fish and steak eatery, had dark wood around the bar, side walls, and high-back booths. Cigar smoke hung in layers, blending twin whiffs of grilled steak and boiled shellfish in its swirls. Stryker and Morgan dined there often.

The maître d' rushed to welcome him. "Good evening, Mister Stryker." Stryker was well known in the grill. Several months before, he helped the owner prevent young hoodlums from robbing the customers. None of the would-be robbers walked out with any money. They all died in the restaurant.

"Not here to eat," Stryker answered.

"Oh, then what can we do for you, sir?"

"The woman, attractive, long dark hair, I usually have with me. She was here four nights ago with three men. She sat at one of the booths. Who were the men?"

Mister Stryker, we don't want any trouble." The maître d' shook his head, looking fearful. He'd watched Stryker kill muggers with deadly efficiency and might have suspected he had a jealous man on his hands.

"Senator Hearst thinks she was kidnapped. She was last seen here at your place." Stryker's eyes narrowed. "Who waited on 'em?"

"Senator Hearst?" The name impressed the maître d'. He relaxed a bit and looked around the room. "I'll see if he's here. He's supposed to come in about now." Stryker figured mentioning Hearst's name would lend itself favorably for the maître d' to be accommodative, perhaps almost much as he would be at the point of a gun.

"Your office back there?" Stryker asked, pointing toward a closed door by the kitchen.

The maître d' nodded. "Mister Kerns is not here tonight, but I think he'd let you use it." Kerns is the owner. It was his shotgun and Stryker's Peacemaker that stopped the robbery that night.

"Send the waiter to me." Stryker started toward the kitchen. There were two reasons why he wanted to interview the waiter in the office. The first was not to be interrupted. Second; the waiter might need *persuasion*. He didn't think he needed to do that, but…. He walked to the back, wove among the busy cooks, and opened the office door.

The owner's office walls were painted a light green. A desk and a swivel chair behind it flanked two straight-back chairs in front. A kerosene lamp hung on a wall, one sat on the desk, and another on shelving next to loose-leaf cookbooks. Stryker sat behind the desk. He didn't have to wait long.

After a knock sounded at the door, Stryker called out, "Come in." A young man in his early twenties cautiously pushed open the door. At five feet tall with short sandy hair and freckles, the smartly dressed waiter had a medium build inside the black short jacketed uniform with a white shirt and a black bowtie. He stood nervously by the desk, acting as if he were about to be admonished for something.

"Sit," Stryker ordered.

The waiter sat.

"What's your name?"

"Jason."

"Four nights ago, you waited on a woman, early thirties, long dark hair, attractive, with three men in one of the booths. She may have been kidnapped. She's disappeared. Tell me everything you know about her and the men, and tell me what you heard them say."

"Not much, sir. I just took their food and drinks order. You might want to speak to Patty. She served them. That's how we do it here. I take the orders. Someone else delivers it. Patty usually works with me on those booths." Jason pointed at the wall as if one could see through it.

"Patty here tonight?" Stryker asked.

Jason nodded. "Want me to go get her?"

"Yes."

Jason leaped to his feet and rushed to the door, flinging it open and rushing out. He returned a minute later with a girl in her mid-twenties. She was plain-looking with hair tied back by a white handkerchief. She wore no make-up and was thirty pounds overweight on a five-four body. Stryker suspected she had achieved her potential. It was a man's world in the 1880s. Patty probably wouldn't move up anyway.

"This is Patty," Jason said. "She can probably tell you more than I can." He turned to leave.

"Don't leave, Jason," Stryker ordered. "Both of you sit." Stryker jabbed a finger at the two chairs. "Close the door, Jason."

Jason, looking none too happy, took a seat. Patty eased into a chair too.

"Patty, Jason tell you what this is about?"

Patty nodded twice.

"Tell me everything you saw and heard at the table that night."

"Well, before I brought the food the men had—"

"How were they seated at the table?" Stryker interrupted.

"Two men sat across the table from the woman and another man."

"Go on."

"They had what looked like a drawing with slanted lines and lines crossing them lines. The man by the woman was pointing at stuff on it. I don't know what any of it meant."

"Anything written on the paper, like a title? What did you tell the police you haven't told me?"

"They asked who might have heard them talking, and I told him their names, the Leonard's. They sat at a table, not a booth, and across from their booth. I think they knew the woman. I saw 'em greet each other."

"How about anything on the paper?" Stryker asked.

"Yes, now I remember," Patty replied, nodding thoughtfully with scrunched eyebrows. "Empire. It said, 'Empire,' up at the top. I remember thinking it was some kind of a kingdom or somethin'. But I thought that was silly thinkin'," Patty chuckled. She glanced sheepishly at Jason. When she turned back to Stryker, her smile vanished.

"Did they mention where they might be going later?"

"No, sir."

"Jason?" Stryker was getting impatient.

"No, sir."

"Empire could be a mining operation. Know anything about that?"

Jason and Patty shook their heads.

"Describe the men," Stryker demanded.

"They weren't wearing suits or nothin'," Jason offered. "I'd say all three were in their mid-forties. They wore beards. Hardy and rugged looking, like maybe they didn't work indoors. Didn't seem like the sun got to 'em, though." Jason glanced at Patty.

"That's about all I can remember, too," Patty added.

"If you see the men, or the woman again, get word to Senator Hearst immediately. He'll be at the Palace Hotel."

"Yes, sir," they answered together. They looked serious enough.

"You can go." Stryker jutted out his chin.

Jason leaped from his chair, scooted out the door, and through the kitchen before Patty left the office.

"Thank you, sir," the girl said, giving Stryker a short curtsy.

Stryker had no idea why Patty bowed. There was nothing regal about him. He suspected if he asked her why, she wouldn't know either. After thanking the maître d', he left the restaurant and headed back to the hotel and Hearst. The senator, having made his fortune in mining, might know something about the Empire Mine.

Stryker was in a hurry. Like other times before when on foot and not with Morgan, he took the shortcut through an alley, but the boots were not made for walking, especially fast walking, and he cursed out loud at the footwear, the uneven stones, and not finding Morgan. It had grown dark. Clouds covered the quarter moon and only defused lantern light from building windows punctured the darkness.

CHAPTER THREE

Stryker crossed California Street and walked past Pine Street when he heard boys talking in an alley. Although he couldn't see them, they sounded like teenagers. Their voices came from deep in the alley between a hardware store and a dry goods shop. Stryker stopped. After his short pause, he started out again carefully placing each boot toe first on the sidewalk. He had no time for trouble that might come from the alley.

He stopped again when he heard one boy talk excitedly about what was in a woman's purse. Stryker edged to the corner.

"There must be over a hundred dollars in here! Holy shit! She musta been rich!"

"Hold it down, dammit!" another one cursed.

Must have been? Morgan? Stryker peeked around the corner. Three male teenagers knelt next to a kerosene lantern, digging through what appeared to be a woman's black handbag. Its contents were spilled onto the cobblestone. *Morgan's purse?* He couldn't see it clearly. He quelled his breathing to listen.

"Rich and pretty. Wish we hadn't killed her."

"We raped her, Phil. She saw us up fucking close, dumb-ass. Wanna hang?"

"Yeah, I know. I just woulda liked to fuck her again."

"She was getting' pretty messed up, face an' all."

"Think they'll find her?"

"Ah, hell no. Not in the fuckin' ocean."

"Yeah, I guess. Been four days now. Ain't heard nothin'."

"Good idea to dump her in the bay wasn't it?"

"Yeah, Jack. I still don't know why we waited to come back for the purse, though. What if someone else hadda found it?

"Okay, fucker! I forgot the damn thing. So did you and Phil! We couldn't come right back. What if somebody seen us kill her? Ever think of that, dipshit?"

"Shhhh, dammit! Hold it down assholes!" The third boy, the unnamed one, cursed in an angry whisper. "Let's hurry up and get the fuck outta here."

"Hey! Here's a picture of her with a man! Phil exclaimed.

"Damn, he's a mean-looking fucker." Jack said, forgetting to not talk out loud.

That was enough for the mixed breed. He charged, covering the fifteen feet to the boys in less than two seconds with his sai in one hand and razor in the other.

He hit two boys as they stood and turned. He cracked the first boy's forehead with the sai handle. The razor slashed the second boy's throat. The kid started to run but fell to the cobblestone with blood spewing from the gash.

Stryker lunged at the third boy and slammed him against the bricks. He placed the sai under the kid's chin, and in a powerful upward thrust, Stryker drove the center tine through the roof of his mouth and into his brain.

Letting the body drop, Stryker returned to the first kid who lay on the cobblestone conscious and groaning loudly. Stryker grabbed him by the hair and jerked his head back. The terrified boy stopped groaning and stared at Stryker. While transfixed by the ghostly pale eyes, the razor sliced his throat.

Kneeling, Stryker searched through the purse contents and found the photograph. He picked it up and held it near the lantern. The woman in the picture wasn't Morgan. Much relieved, Stryker left the alley and hurried to the Palace.

A few days later, the stinking bodies of the boys were discovered. The police speculated it was the work of a crazed killer or that of a savage animal. Hard to say, they said. The decomposed bodies left the cuts ragged, maggot-infested cavities. The police were correct on the first speculation and damn close on the second.

In the hotel lobby, Stryker ordered the desk clerk to call for Senator Hearst. Stryker heard the senator in the speaking tube say for him to come up immediately, and he rushed off.

"Sir, you can…," the clerk turned to Stryker but he was already halfway across the lobby.

"What do you know about the Empire Mine?" Stryker asked, entering the room.

"It's a gold mine in Grass Valley, California," Hearst replied. "Located over in Nevada County. There's some gold in it, a lot of gold, I reckon. That is, if they can get it out. A fellow by the name of Bill Bourn bought it about eighteen years ago and was doing all right 'til he ran into a flooding problem. Heard he was bringing in a Cornish engine to pump water outta the mine shaft." Hearst's face brightened. "Starr, that Leonard couple said they heard that name mentioned. He's a cousin of Bourn, supposed to be a mining engineer expert. Come to think of it, Stryker, Morgan knows a lot about the Cornish pump."

"Morgan take off to work with 'em without telling you? Stryker's eyes narrowed in a frown.

"No, no, she wouldn't. Not unless she went against her will, Stryker." Hearst returned the scowl with a grimace of his own. "I know Bourn. He doesn't strike me as a man who'd kidnap a woman," Hearst said, shaking his head.

"They were the last people to see her." Stryker chose not to mention the alley incident. If those three boys raped or killed Morgan in a separate attack, he'd never know it now. He ruefully realized he should have kept one alive to question. "Shit!" he said aloud.

"Yeah, shit, Stryker." Hearst had no idea they weren't talking about the same shit.

"Did she get on a train?"

"Not that I know of," Hearst replied, shaking his head. "But I'll send a man down to the Ferry House. Maybe someone saw her leave."

"I'll go," Stryker said. "If anyone knows where she went, I'll board the next train. Otherwise, I'll go see Estelle's sister," Stryker said over his shoulder as he headed out the door.

"Hold on, Stryker." Hearst went to a wingback chair and picked up a quill pen and writing paper. He dipped the pen in ink, wrote something, and signed his name. When finished, Hearst creased the paper in three folds and handed it to Stryker. "If you need someone to help you, show them this."

Stryker took the letter and stuffed it in his shirt pocket. It was only later, after leaving the senator, that he read what Hearst wrote.

I will be much obliged if you would provide Mister Stryker with whatever assistance he might ask of you.

Sincerely, George Hearst
United States Senator.

Twenty-five minutes later, Stryker swung off the cable car at the Ferry House. Cable cars ran on a rotating circular platform to turn them around. He jumped off as it was still turning. He pushed through a crowd of men and women by the turn table, then steadied himself on the fixed planks before rushing to the ticket booths.

Shit. Long lines of people crowded in front of the nine ticket windows. Stryker *politely* shoved people out of his way to get to the front of a line. Women squealed, men cursed, but none challenged the the .44.

"What trains pulled out of here after nine o'clock four nights ago? And where to?" Stryker yelled at the startled ticket agent. They kept no passenger records, so it was a slim chance to learn if Morgan boarded a train.

The agent slipped Stryker the schedule sheets showing times and routes. It showed eighteen stops south toward San Jose. Another sheet had ferry times across the bay to Vallejo and on up to Sacramento. *Fuck.* He turned away from the window. There was no use asking the nine ticket window clerks if they remembered a particular woman, even if she was a good-looking woman, boarding a train. *Fuck!*

He fingered the senator's note in his pocket and looked at the schedule again. *Wait... times.* He ran his finger over the times in the late evening. Only three trains left between nine o'clock and midnight. All three ran through San Jose, two continued south with stops toward San Diego. One turned north through Stockton and Sacramento and moved across the Sierras going east. It also had stops in smaller towns. *Did a line branch from Colfax to Grass Valley and the Empire Mine?*

Stryker pushed his way to the front of a ticket line again, ignoring grumblings and complaints. Again, no one tried to stop him.

"Yes sir, mister," the flustered clerk said, responding to Stryker's shouted inquiry. "The Nevada County Railroad Company runs a line to Nevada City."

The next scheduled departure to Sacramento and on to Colfax had a departure in ninety minutes. Stryker got in line to buy a ticket. This time he queued up in the rear of a line. He bought a ticket for himself and one for the roan. Someone at the smaller stations in San Jose and Colfax might remember Morgan.

After buying tickets, Stryker politely lined up at the deli counter and bought a ham sandwich and a mug of coffee. He found a stand-up table to eat the sandwich and drink the coffee. He still had time to buy and read the *San Francisco Examiner* from front to back. He searched the personals, knowing there would be no notice from Morgan, and of course, there was none. There wasn't a ransom notice either. He wrote a note to tell Hearst his plans on paper he got from the deli. Stryker hailed a horse cab, gave the driver a dollar, and handed him the note for the senator at the Palace Hotel. Ordinarily, he wouldn't tell Hearst of his travel plans, but this time he did. The old man was genuinely worried... *and dammit*, he was too.

A half-hour before the train departure, the station hostler brought up the roan. The horse shook its head angrily, almost whipping the lead rope out of the man's hand. Stryker figured maybe the roan wasn't eager to get on the trail again after a hard ride over the mountains. Both of them were in bad moods.

Stryker watched the horse get loaded in the Mather stock car, and then he followed to ensure it had food and water. Once settled, he queued up with the rest of the passengers to board the Pullman car. Angling his way through the travelers, he moved to the front of the line. Stryker wanted to get his usual seat facing forward in the rear. Some sleeping berths were available on the Pullman; however, he preferred to sit where he could keep a watchful eye on his things. Although at times, his watchful eye dozed off. Since the passenger count was light, Stryker assumed he would have the rear area to himself, but he was wrong. A man, about five-foot-ten with an average build and sporting a full beard and a well-tailored suit, made his way down the aisle and took the padded seat opposite Stryker.

Shit, he'll probably want to talk.

It wasn't until the train was well on its run to San Jose, having made three stops already in San Bruno, Burlingame, and San Mateo before the passenger said anything to the long-legged man with the Stetson pulled over his brow.

"Mind if I ask where you're going tonight." The man sounded friendly and correctly guessed Stryker wasn't sleeping.

Stryker raised the hat brim with a forefinger. "Don't know yet."

"Are you running from something?"

"No."

"I am. I guess I've been running from something all my life," the fellow said, staring absently out a dark window. "My name's Robert, by the way."

Stryker ignored the introduction and started to lower his hat again, but then Robert added, "They wanted me to run for president, but I turned them down."

"Stryker," Stryker surprised himself by offering his name.

"Excuse me, sir?"

"My name."

"Oh." Robert leaned forward as if to extend a hand and then noticed the grim features of the mixed breed. He settled back on the seat. "I served as Secretary of War under Presidents Garfield and Arthur until three years ago. Now they want me to be minister to Great Britain. I might take that job. I don't want anything more to do with Cabinet positions and being abroad for a while might do me some good."

Stryker thought this Robert fellow was full of shit. He kept the thought to himself and said nothing. He had a mental picture of throwing Robert off the train, but that would probably delay finding Morgan, so he let Robert talk.

"Ah well," Robert continued. "I like this train. George Pullman sure improved traveling on rails, don't you think?" He patted the velvet seat beside him. He's asked me to serve as his legal counsel. I might do that sometime in the future, maybe after the minister's job. By the way, I'm a lawyer. I don't know, but I think I would like riding around the country on one of these." Robert smiled and patted the cushion again.

A pompous ass, that's how Stryker figured the man. *Either that or a silly, self-absorbed faker.* He didn't know how much more he could stand. He was about to say, "Shut the fuck up," when Robert shrugged his shoulders and said, "Stryker, I've been living in my father's shadows all my life. Never good enough. Wherever I went, whatever I did, it was always people wanting me to be my father, not myself. I can't get away from it. I suppose you wouldn't know what that is like, people always expecting you to live up to the image of a great man, and then displaying their disappointment no matter how hard you tried. In my own right, I suppose I've done okay. Nothing great, mind you, but okay, I guess. A life of frustration, though. That's why I might take the job with Pullman. It would get me out of the public's eye, and I could just do boring work where greatness isn't expected. Now, I suppose I've bent your ear enough. Please excuse me if I try to catch a few winks." Robert rose, gave Stryker a polite nod, and walked past him through the thick curtains to the sleeping berths.

Stryker didn't have to shut him up or throw him from the train. He never learned who the man was, never knew if he was a fake, and never saw him again.

Robert's father had been assassinated in Ford's theater on April 15, 1865. Oddly, a year or two prior, Robert Todd Lincoln had his own life saved from being run over by a train. The man who saved his life was Edwin Booth, brother of John Wilkes Booth.

Robert did take the job with Pullman.

Stryker sat alone, dozing on and off as the train made four more stops. Thirty-nine minutes after Robert left to find his sleeping berth, the train arrived at the Market Street Station in San Jose. Stryker didn't see Robert get off the train and figured he must have continued south.

At the station, Stryker stepped from the Southern Pacific train, retrieved the roan, tied it to a rail, and went inside to find the Central Pacific shedules to Sacramento and Colfax, which had recently merged with the Southern Pacific Line. The upright clock in the corner read eleven o'clock. The schedule board on the wall showed the next train left for Sacramento at 5:10 a.m. He went back outside to stable the roan for the next few hours. The hulking Consolidation locomotive's drive rods turned the driver wheels as the big engine slowly pulled forward. Stryker stopped a moment and watched it blow white steam billows in the dark as it left the station. Then he took the roan off the platform and around the corner of the station. There was no lantern light behind the building, so he stopped to let his eyes adjust. Gas streetlights down Market Street lit building fronts of mostly brick these days. Some were single-story and some multi-story. San Jose was a bustling town with a population of over twelve thousand, but the dusty streets were deserted tonight. At least, that's what Stryker thought.

He led the roan around the corner and then he was jumped by four men. Two grabbed his arms. Two pulled his legs out from under him. With his back and on the ground, his arms were pinned by two men, and he could only fight with his legs.

Stryker knee kicked and leg swept the two standing men. Then one threw himself across Stryker's ankles, pinning his legs on the ground. Stryker kicked free and clamped his legs around the man's middle in a crushing scissor clinch.

"Ahhh! Can't breathe, Joel."

Joel was the man still standing. "Amos! Dammit! Hold his fucking arm down!" Joel yelled, kicking Stryker's ribs.

Amos threw his upper body on Stryker's arm. "Lay on it, Rico!"

Amos tightened the grip on the Stryker's wrist, cursing, "Bastard's fightin' hard!"

With two men pinning down his arms, and his legs locked around a third, Joel was free to kick Stryker. Each pointed bootkick cracked a rib.

Then, Joel leaped up and aimed to kick Stryker's face.

Stryker remained rolled up his right hip concealing the holstered Colt, but that was all he could do before passing out. Joel kicked Stryker's face a few more times and growled, "Check his pockets, Nate. Gonna look in the saddle bags."

Nate pried Stryker's legs off and caught his breath, before swinging around to straddle Stryker's thighs. Stryker had paper dollars and coins in the left pocket. Nate had gotten the dollars out when Joel screamed.

The roan, a loyal horse to the mixed breed, reared up and attacked his assailants to protect his master. Well all right, it didn't happen exactly that way. The commotion spooked the roan, and when Joel tried to grab the reins, it reared and flailed its steel hooves. One struck Joel's forehead, crushing the frontal bone. The man died before he hit the ground.

"Hey Joel, you all right?"

When he failed to answer, Nate jumped to his feet and ran to his cohort. Dropping to one knee, he turned Joel's head and saw the ghastly wound. "Joel's dead," Nate deadpanned.

"Shit! What do we do now, Nate?" cried Amos, still lying on Stryker's arm.

"Yeah, Nate," yelled Rico. He slapped Stryker's face. No response. "He's still out."

Nate stood and stared at Joel's body. "We can't leave Joel here." He came back to Amos and Rico, who were now on their feet. "They'll know it was us."

"What about him?" one of them asked, pointing to Stryker.

"Leave him. We got his money."

They decided to leave the skittish roan, but not before trying and failing to put Joel's body on it.

Joel was buried two days later. People paid their last respects to him even though he was not all that well-liked. It was said he got kicked by his own horse. Maybe the horse didn't care for him either, some said.

Hours later, night yielded to a cloudy gray morning.

"Is he dead?"

"He looks like shit."

"See if he's breathing, Jack."

Jack was one of three school kids who found Stryker by the depot on their way to school. The two boys and one girl were all in the academy. Jack moved closer and knelt next to the injured man. He leaned over and placed his ear next to Stryker's mouth. Stryker groaned. Jack recoiled, letting out a high-pitched scream, and he landed on his backside. The other two kids burst out laughing.

"Yeah, he's alive," the girl chuckled.

"We better get to school," the boy next to the girl said. "Let's go. We can tell Mrs. Brixey."

Stryker struggled to open his swollen eyes when two San Jose deputies showed up. His eyes were stuck together with congealed blood. One wouldn't open at all. He felt his face. His nose was swollen and misshaped. He could feel the bare cheekbone on the right side of his face. He looked down and saw blood soaking his shirt. He ran his tongue around his teeth and none felt loose. He touched his mouth and felt the lips were numb and swollen. His face was a bloody mess.

"Hey, mister. What the hell happened to you?"

"Got jumped," Stryker said tried sitting up. Searing pain in the ribs stopped that. He lay back before trying it again.

"Busted ribs?"

"Yeah."

"Know who did it?"

"No."

"See if you can get him on his feet, Bill."

"I can get up myself," Stryker growled. He rolled to all fours and stood, but the pain in his ribs made it difficult to breathe. He couldn't hide it. Stryker had been shot before, broken bones too, but the most painful injury he ever experienced was a broken rib, and now it felt as if he had several. *Can't move, hurts to breathe, can't sleep, and can't get in a position to ease the pain. And yeah, better not cough or sneeze cause it's gonna hurt like hell.*

"Can you ride?" Bill asked.

"Reckon." Stryker weazed.

"Head down to San Carlos Street." The deputy pointed a finger. "Turn left on it. "In about a half mile turn right on Di Salvo and that'll take you to the O'Conner Sanitarium. Just opened last year. They've turned it into a hospital now and they have doctors there. You oughta to go see 'em," the deputy advised. The name tag on his left pocket read, "Delford."

Stryker had missed the five ten train and needed medical attention, so he nodded.

"Here's your hat, mister." Bill picked up the Stetson and brushed it off before handing it to Stryker.

Stryker lifted his arm to put on the hat, but a stab of rib pain curtailed that. He dipped his head and fitted on the Stetson by bending his elbow. He never understood why it hurt like hell to raise his arm with broken ribs. He stumbled thirty feet to the roan munching grass under a maple tree. It took considerable effort and Stryker couldn't stifle the loud groan as he climbed into the saddle. He headed the roan down the street, keeping the roan at a slow walk, but even a measured pace jolted his ribs. Leaning forward, he rested his elbows on the saddle horn, but that was no good either. Three-quarters of a mile is a long way when in severe pain. He turned on San Carlos Street. A half mile more, he turned right on Di Salvo and saw the two-story brick hospital building. It was a welcomed sight. He made a slow, painful dismount, draped the reins over a rail, and climbed the ten steps to the hospital entrance. *Why the hell didn't they put the first floor on ground level?*

"Better get a wheelchair!" someone shouted. Stryker didn't see the woman who shouted, but he was grateful. The steps did him in. The rib pain wouldn't let him catch his breath and he was about to pass out. Two sets of hands caught him before he collapsed on the marble floor.

He woke on a hospital bed, lying naked under a cotton sheet covering him to his hips. The white room had two windows, one opposite the door, and the other on a side wall, which were both open to allow ventilation and sunlight. White linen curtains danced lazily in the breeze. A silver-haired male stood over him examining the purplish bruises on

Stryker's ribs. A nurse, in a white lab coat watched the examination. She stood on the same side as Stryker's swollen eye. She had a trim figure and might have been in her mid-thirties. Yeah, might have been, he couldn't see her very well.

"You've got some fractured ribs there, fella," the doctor said. "You're pretty banged up. What happened to you?"

"Got jumped." Swollen lips muffled Stryker's speech.

"Have you coughed up any blood?"

"No."

"What's your name?"

"Stryker."

"Well, Mister Stryker, I felt a couple of indentations. Could be broken ribs. Ever break 'em before?

"Yes."

"Left side?"

"Both sides."

"Hmmm, well then, I can't tell if these are new or not. If they're not new breaks, judging by your pain, you cracked 'em, or they are badly bruised. Regardless, you'll be in considerable pain for a while." The badge pinned on the white lab coat indicated Dr. Wainwright was his attending physician. He was a thin man of average height. His thinning hair was almost white; Stryker placed him in his early sixties, maybe. He had intelligent blue eyes. "We can tape 'em up to reduce the pain, but you run the risk of getting pneumonia. I saw a lot of men get it during the war when we wrapped them. Your face could use some stitches, too." The doctor picked up the clipboard hanging on the foot rail.

He was still writing when Stryker interrupted. "I'm traveling. I need to get back on the job." Stryker slurred the words, spitting as he talked. "My horse is in front. I need to care for him."

"I'll get someone to stable him. You need to remain here for a few days to make sure those ribs don't move and puncture a lung. You won't last long if you do. You need to sleep sitting up; I'm not gonna tape you, so I'll give you something for pain." The doctor continued scribbling on the clipboard. He wrote as he spoke to his nurse. "Jennifer, send for a shot of morphine. Give it to Mister Stryker, then suture that cut." He pointed his pen at Stryker's face. "And clean him up."

"Yes, doctor." Jennifer did an about-face that would have impressed a drill sergeant and marched from the room.

"I'll check on you this afternoon," Doctor Wainwright said. "By the way, I don't care what you did to get in here." He released the clipboard and it banged against the footrail, and then he left.

A few minutes later, Nurse Jennifer re-entered pushing a wheeled cart. She parked it next to Stryker's bed, where Stryker could see the suture needle and thread, a carbolic acid bottle, a jar of cotton balls, a towel, and a bowl of water. Next to the tray, a hypodermic needle and a small vial lay on a white cotton cloth.

"I'll give you a shot to ease the pain first." Nurse Jennifer picked up the needle and vial. She filled the needle and then squirted a little out to eliminate air bubbles. "You want it in your behind or arm? It's got to be in a muscle." Nurse Jennifer did not smile.

"Arm."

"As Nurse Jennifer prepared to administer the shot, she told him, "You look like you got French-kissed by a freight train. Give me your arm."

Stryker lifted his arm. *Shit, that hurt.* He wondered what his face looked like.

After giving Stryker the shot, Nurse Jennifer left the room and returned in fifteen minutes. It took about that long for Stryker to feel dizzy and weightless. The pain was gone, though.

"Let's sew you up. Scoot to the edge of the bed."

Stryker did as he was instructed; the move was painless. With the pain alleviated, his mind was able to think of other things, like Jennifer. Her hair was pinned back on both sides. She looked to be all business, but without the hairpins, she could have been more attractive. Then he reproached himself. *What the hell are you thinking, asshole? You need to find Morgan.*

When Nurse Jennifer swabbed his face with the antiseptic her hands were gentle. She put a stitch on each end of the cut and then closed it with six more. Afterward, she cleaned the dried blood from his face and applied ice in a towel to his swollen eye. Stryker did not ask her where she got the ice but he found out later the hospital had it delivered from the ice plant near the railroad station.

"You've had a rough life, Mister Stryker," Nurse Jennifer said, running a soft hand over his numerous welts and scars. "What kind of work do you do?"

"Odd jobs."

"Hmmm, they've taken a toll."

"Give me pain medication when I leave."

Nurse Jennifer glared at Stryker's pale eyes, taking a moment to consider the request. "The doctor may give you something in five days."

"One day."

"Convince the doctor," she said matter of factly.

"A woman's life is in danger."

"Your ribs are bad."

"Why I want medication. I'm leaving tomorrow," he argued.

"You could puncture a lung."

"She could die."

"All right. I'll get you a few cocaine pills. They'll fire me if I'm found out. Don't know why I should help you, but I believe you when you say a woman is in trouble."

Maybe she did believe him, maybe she didn't. For whatever reason, the hard-assed nurse chose to risk it. "This woman… does she mean something to you?" Nurse Jennifer asked with a trace of hesitation.

"She works for Senator Hearst," Stryker replied. He narrowed his eyes.

"I think she means something to you."

"She saved my life," Stryker added. He figured there was no need to throw his affections for Morgan in Jennifer's face. He needed her help.

"Senator Hearst. You work for him too?"

"Odd jobs."

"I see." Nurse Jennifer took the cart and started for the door.

"Leaving early, around four," Stryker called after her.

Nurse Jennifer looked back, nodded, and left the room.

"Don't go yet," Stryker called out.

Nurse Jennifer stepped back into the room.

"Where's my clothes?"

"See you in the morning," Nurse Jennifer said breezily, and she left.

"Early!" Stryker called after her. He wasn't sure she heard him. The morphine had taken full effect and his eyelids were heavy. He settled down into the bed, not all the way flat, and he was careful not to scrunch the ribs. He took deep breaths. He'd heard about pneumonia with broken ribs before.

His eyelids settled together, and he let them stay that way. He slept most of the day. Sometime during the afternoon, Nurse Jennifer and Doctor Wainwright came in and she gave him another morphine shot. Their motive may have been to keep him in bed more than for the pain, but it was probably both. Regardless, Stryker was half awake when they came in, and he did not put up a struggle. He fell back asleep almost immediately, and Nurse Jennifer lingered a while after the doctor left, gazing at the man she knew nothing about. Strangely, the tall man whose legs stretched past the end of the bed piqued her interest. "You're not all that handsome, Stryker."

After several hours of deep sleep, Stryker drifted to a lighter slumber, where dreams come alive.

Leigh

She was in the kitchen of the New York apartment. She had her back to him, cooking on the stove. The walls were all white. Natural pine cabinets. The sink was next to the stove. A window was over the sink. It was early evening. Still light. A pot with a handle sat on the stove, simmering potpourri. Couldn't smell it.

Leigh turned and talked without moving her lips, the way people do in dreams. "I don't have the right spices."

She wore an apron over a flowered dress. Her blond hair was swept behind her ears. She looked so beautiful. He ached so bad for her.

"What do you need?" Stryker's mouth didn't move either.

"I don't know. I can't find what's missing." She talked illogically like people sometimes do in dreams.

"Leigh, I thought you died," Stryker said.

"No, I was alive, but you left me. Why, Stryker? Why did you leave me?"

"Leigh, you died in the meadow. I held you. You died."

"No Stryker. You left me. I cried. You rode away," Leigh said crying.

The dream lingered like bad dreams do.

Stryker felt helpless and guilty. *I failed her. God help me. Help her.* Leigh had cried. *She knew I killed her that day in the meadow. I should have checked the firing coordinates. That damn artillery shell ripped her apart. Please, God! Bring her back. It won't happen again. No, it won't, asshole, cause she's gone. Gone forever. Asshole.*

"Here are your clothes, Stryker." Nurse Jennifer stood beside his bed. The early morning sun had yet to lighten the room.

Stryker opened his eyes. Nurse Jennifer was silhouetted in lantern light from the hallway.

"Your gun, too. I suppose you'll need it."

"On the bed," Stryker mumbled, struggling to extricate himself from the dream and respond coherently. *Damn, nightmares.* He tried sitting up but the rib pain stopped that. "Ah… shit," he cursed through clenched teeth.

"Here's your pills, too." Nurse Jennifer placed the clothing and Colt on the bed beside Stryker and pulled out a small bottle of pills from her jacket pocket.

Stryker reached for the bottle, twisted off the metal cap, and poured out a pill, swallowing it without water. "Thanks."

"I'll help you." Using two hands on Stryker's arm, Nurse Jennifer pulled him up and he swung his feet to the floor.

"Why?"

"I don't know. Don't ask me that." Nurse Jennifer offered a fractured smile.

Stryker reached for his trousers and slid in one leg at a time, trying not to bend over. He put on his shirt, carefully. The socks and boots would be a problem. He stood and carried them to a straight-back chair near the bed. He dropped the boots and sat down. Propping an ankle across a knee, he worked on a sock. He got the other sock on. Then reached for a boot. "Aaah!" The medication hadn't had time to work. He sat upright, taking quick short breaths.

"Sit back. Give me your foot." Nurse Jennifer knelt and picked up the boot. She worked it onto his foot as far as she could. "Now push."

Stryker shoved his foot the rest of the way in the boot.

"Give me your other foot." Together, they worked on the boot. Stryker got to his feet, picked up his gun belt, and put it around his waist. He had to lower his head again to put on the damn hat.

"Where's my horse?"

"The stable is out the front entrance on the right. Not far, maybe a hundred feet. It sets back from the street. Here, don't forget these." Nurse Jennifer grabbed the pill bottle from off the bed and handed it to Stryker. "Those stitches will need to come out in seven days."

Stryker stuffed the bottle in his shirt pocket. He dug out a ten-dollar gold coin and handed it to Nurse Jennifer. "Pay the doctor."

He started for the door. Nurse Jennifer slid in front of him, stood on her toes, kissed his stitches, and then disappeared from the room. Stryker paused a moment at the door, staring down the empty hallway.

CHAPTER FOUR

Stryker walked from the hospital. The painkiller allowed a brisker pace. He found the stable where Nurse Jennifer said it was. It sat further back from the street than he expected, but that was only a minor irritation. He wondered how he would be on the roan. The ribs had hurt like hell before the medication and he was still dazed from having the shit kicked out of him. He thought about meeting up with the shit-kickers again, but not yet. Once inside the stable, he found the roan in the third stall on the left. Its blanket and saddle were hung on a rail. Good for the horse. Not so good for him, and there was no one in the livery at such an early hour. *Shit.*

Stryker thought about Morgan's possible condition. He pulled the bottle from his pocket, opened it, and poured the pills on the ground. He ground them in the dirt with a boot and tossed away the bottle. After placing the blanket on the roan, he clenched his teeth and picked up the saddle. He gritted harder and with a loud grunt, got the saddle on the roan. Cinching the girth and putting on the bridle felt less painful. *Maybe the pills are starting to work.* He led the horse from the stall and out of the stable before mounting. It was still dark outside when he met a stable boy starting his early chores.

Stryker tugged the reins, stopping by the youngster. "What I owe for the horse?"

"If you paid the hospital, you don't owe anything. It's part of the hospital bill. They said you was hurt and would be in there several days."

"I paid 'em." Stryker bumped his heels on the roan's flanks to start down the street. He wondered how much he would regret throwing away the pills. It was half past four when he turned onto San Carlos Street. The train to Sacramento was scheduled to leave at five ten. He had time.

Approaching the station, Stryker pulled the Colt. Dawn was an hour away. He had no time for another mugging or another attempted mugging. No *would-be* muggers stood behind the station anyway. He rode around front where the train engine was billowing steam, and dismounted. He stepped on the platform and crossed the planks to the ticket window. Lantern light lit up the office and he could see the ticket agent moving inside.

"Got delayed yesterday and missed the train." Stryker pushed the unused tickets, one for him, one for the roan, under the window's iron bars. "Need 'em exchanged."

The agent stood with his back to the ticket window. "Too bad, mister," he said, without turning around.

Stryker pulled the Peacemaker, shoved its barrel between the bars, and clunked the iron. "Exchange the tickets."

"I told you—," The agent said. He was a portly man in his early fifties, wearing a white pin-striped shirt and suspenders. He spun around and gazed at Stryker, and then at the .44. "Looks like you had an accident. And yes, an exchange is in order." He picked up the unused tickets, read them, and threw them in a waste basket. "You and your horse to Colfax," he said tearing off new tickets. All right, mister. Here you are. Have a pleasant trip."

Stryker took the tickets and holstered the Colt. "Got coffee inside," Stryker asked in his customary, often irritating, statement.

"Freshly made pot on a table. Help yourself." A gun pointed at a fellow can make a man friendlier.

It was a quarter to five. No passengers waited on the platform which was dimly lit with lantern light from the office. Stryker stepped inside the station. The pine-paneled room was thirty feet square with rows of partially empty benches ready for waiting passengers. To Stryker's right, an open window led to the ticket agent. Eight people rested on the benches, two couples appeared to be in their early forties, and four men sat by themselves. The coffee urn sat on a wooden table by the back wall and Stryker cut a path for the brew. After picking off a white porcelain mug from the stack and filling it, he sipped coffee and surveyed the room. A slender stern-looking man seated next to a woman, presumably his wife, glanced up from his newspaper and nodded a greeting. Stryker returned a mug salute. The other passengers remained occupied and to themselves. He'd almost finished the coffee when the conductor leaned into the doorway and called, "All aboard!"

Stryker downed the last of the coffee and followed the other passengers out to the train. When he boarded, he found the coach almost full. With paneled walls and cushioned bench seats, he thought about how train travel was changing in the 1880s. He started down the center aisle and saw a man and woman seated in the next to last row. *Shit.* Rather than trying another coach, he made his way to an empty seat in the back row. It faced forward and was beside a large matronly woman and a large velvet carry bag. Stryker picked up the bag and dropped it on the woman's lap. He ignored her scornful look as he sat beside her. Then he turned to the woman and returned her scowl with a menacing pale-eyed glare. She quickly opened the bag as if searching for something and eventually withdrew a book. The sun had yet to peep over the mountains, and the woman would need excellent eyesight to see the print. Nevertheless, she opened the book and mouthed words. Wall lanterns burned whale oil that provided some light, probably not good for reading, though. Stryker squared himself away from her encroaching rump and lowered the Stetson.

An hour and a half passed. The train made stops in Pleasanton and Dublin. At Dublin, it turned east. Stryker lifted the hat brim and gazed out the window, watching the landscape slip by before allowing his eyes to settle on the couple across from him. The diminutive girl was an attractive young thing in her late teens or early twenties. She had short dark hair and offered him a fractured smile. The train whistle blew at a railroad crossing as she opened her mouth to speak. It was a long whistle and the girl lost her nerve to start a conversation. She peered out the window instead.

"Where might you be traveling, sir?" The man seated next to her asked.

"Colfax." Stryker figured the couple as man and wife. The girl watched him, showing interest in what he had to say. Stryker kept his eyes on the man. He was a thin-faced, sharp-boned fellow with a well-trimmed mustache. Even at a young age, his countenance suggested it had been a while since he had cracked a smile. He thought it was an odd couple.

"My name is Flora, my husband's name is Elias." Flora regained her courage now that her husband had broken the ice. Elias sat silent, swaying with the car's rocking, and he let his wife carry the conversation. "And you are mister...?"

"Stryker."

"Stryker, did you have an accident?"

His stitches and bruises must have begged for an explanation. "Close enough." Stryker shifted his attention to Elias.

Elias returned a mirthless stare. He was a none-too-friendly fellow, not that Stryker cared. He looked back at the girl.

"We're traveling back to Chicago. Are you traveling far?" Flora asked.

"Just to Colfax."

"Do you mind if I ask what kind of work you do?"

Inquisitive little thing. "Odd jobs."

"You're like my husband. Flora flashed her smile again. "Elias does odd..." she glanced at her husband. "Elias can do many things. He's..."

"A contractor and entrepreneur," Elias clipped. "I work mostly for myself."

The man seemed to take umbrage at being someone who worked odd jobs.

He continued, "We managed a hotel in Florida for a while and recently left that to come out to California. Thinking of moving to Chicago now." Elias crossed his legs and patted Flora's thigh.

"Elias helped build the railroad across Colorado and was a professional fiddle player in Denver. He's a very good musician." Flora, like many dutiful and loving wives, sought to bolster her husband's image. "We just got married this year." Flora took her husband's hand, squeezed it, and gave him an adoring smile.

They made Stryker recall his early marriage with Leigh. Although he couldn't muster a favorable expression to offer the couple, he envied their young lives together. He did offer a nod.

The conversation continued off and on for many miles. The train stopped in Stockton for passengers and to take on water for the boiler. During the stop, Elias, Flora, and Stryker exited the coach for personal needs and to stretch their legs. Stryker bought a mug of coffee and a sausage biscuit in the station deli. He ate and drank by himself. Elias and Flora had tea and crumpets in the same deli but at another table. However, when they re-boarded they took the same seats exchanging sociable, brief words occasionally. Flora took it upon herself to carry the conversation. The fat woman plumped her *ample ass* in the second coach and Stryker had the back seat to himself.

Not much of note took place between Stryker, Elias, and Flora. Stryker learned that Elias came from Canada and followed Flora's family to Florida to woo the daughter. Flora had a little bump in her belly and wondered if she was pregnant.

Flora asked Stryker more about his being hurt after watching how he walked and sat. It was not difficult to tell Stryker was in pain. He told her he had sore ribs and nothing else was asked, or said, about his injury. The train made another lengthy stop in Sacramento where they disembarked for twenty minutes. When they pulled into Colfax, Stryker rose and tipped his Stetson before he left the coach. They never saw each other again.

Elias and Flora went on with their lives until Flora died in 1938 and Elias in 1941. There was nothing particularly extraordinary about them. Elias worked in construction, becoming a contractor for several years, trying his hand at farming and failed at it. He bought a newspaper route at one time. He and Flora did have five children, four boys and one girl. Two of the boys, Walter and Roy, Roy, born in 1893, and Walter, born in

1901, ran the paper route for Elias. They delivered 600 papers in the morning and 700 papers in the evening. Because of the time required, Walter had poor grades in school. Walter liked to draw and much to the dislike of Elias, he pursued it, drawing animals mostly. At one point he drew a horse for pay. As a result, Elias and his son had a strained relationship, and Elias was not shy about using his belt on the boy.

Eventually, Walter left home. At first, he attempted to join the army to fight in World War I; however, he was turned down because of his young age. Instead, Walter became an ambulance driver, but by the time he got to Europe, the war had ended.

Walter continued with his drawing. He and Roy moved to California and opened an art studio, working as commercial artists. It was tough going for the two young men. They went out of business time and time again. At one point they secured a contract to provide artwork for one hundred dollars a month, but that also failed. Relentlessly, Walter kept at it. Drawing animals was his favorite subject, for years, but it was always without much success.

Then one day in 1928, Walter Elias Disney, drew a mouse.

CHAPTER FIVE

Stryker walked the roan down the cattle ramp and tethered it to a hitching rail. The station housed the ticket office and a gift shop. A statue of Schuyler Colfax who was Speaker of the House in 1865 stood next to the yellow-painted station. A plaque below it was inscribed with Colfax being asked by President Lincoln to dedicate the mining town. It also described how Colfax traveled 2000 miles to the town. Supposedly, he rode 2000 miles on the return trip, too. Lincoln had been shot earlier that year, and Colfax may have felt a special duty to carry out the President's request. Behind the station and across the street, restaurants, cafes, and more gift shops were open and ready to serve. Houses and stores looked well-kept and freshly painted. One could see Colfax was progressing toward quaint.

Stryker entered the station. The sign over the ticket window read "Tickets and Telegrams." Stryker stepped to the window. "A few days ago, some miners returned from San Francisco. They have a woman with them?" Stryker asked the female ticket agent. Stryker hadn't seen a woman working at a train station before. *Times are changing*, he thought. *Next thing you know, they'll be clamoring to vote.*

"I am just back from vacation," the gray-haired, middle-aged woman replied with a friendly smile. "You might ask the girls in the gift shop."

Two women in the gift shop were also middle-aged with graying hair. They stood together chatting and offered welcoming grins to Stryker when he approached. Stryker repeated the question to both women.

"Yes, I remember a woman, one of them supplied." Stryker thought she wasn't too bad for a woman past her prime. She added, "I think she was with a man who owned a mine. I forget his name. He talked like he was the owner. Called it his mine, anyway."

"What did the woman look like?"

"Attractive, with brunette hair. I'd say down to her shoulders. Slim figure," the second girl offered.

"Thanks, girls." Stryker saluted with a finger on the Stetson and turned to walk out.

"Come back soon!" they called after him, but not in unison.

Stryker returned to the ticket window. "Train to Grass Valley?" The female agent flashed another broad smile. *Why is everyone so friendly?*

"The Nevada County Rail Line runs from here through Grass Valley and on to Nevada City, yes," the ticket agent answered without losing the smile. "About seventeen miles to Grass Valley. Would you like a ticket?"

"Yes. And for my horse. I also want to send two telegrams."

"Where to and what do you want to say?"

"Send one to George Hearst at the Palace Hotel in San Francisco. 'Headed to Grass Valley. Morgan may be there. Stryker.'"

"Send the second to the Bank of California in San Francisco. Tell them to wire two hundred dollars to—what's the name of the bank here?"

"State Bank of Cookeville, at the present," The female agent answered. "Peoples State Bank of Colfax is in the works but at the present, the Cookeville bank is run by a man named Mark Cleary. He's a reputable man, although he enjoys life," she giggled.

Stryker wondered if that meant the red-light district in town. Colfax did have a red-light district in the 1880s. After all, it was a mining town. Mark being a devout husband, did not partake in pleasures of the flesh outside of marriage. "Sign the telegram, 'Neville Stryker.' I expect to be back this way in a few days. Tell Cleary that."

"Of course." The agent counted the words with her finger. "That will be three dollars and ninety-five cents. The extra forty-five cents for giving Mark your message."

Stryker slipped a ten-dollar gold coin under the brass bars of the window. "Give change back in paper money. Keep the nickel."

The Nevada County train was a Baldwin locomotive with two coach cars, a cattle car, and a caboose. It sat on a side rail waiting to move on the narrow-gauge rails leading out of Colfax. After the Central Pacific left town, the Nevada County train pulled in front of the station for boarding passengers. Stryker went behind the station to use the facilities and returned as the train pulled up to the boarding platform. He boarded the second coach car and took his usual seat on the most rearward bench. It faced forward. This train had none of the niceties of the Pullman, which meant no cushioned seats. However, the trip to Grass Valley would only take a little over an hour. He watched out the window as the roan and work mules were led into the cattle car.

The coach filled up with miners and wanna-be miners, men who'd heard about gold being dug from the earth around Grass Valley and they flocked to Nevada County to find their fortune. The two biggest mines in the area were the Empire Mine, which Stryker heard about, and the North Star Mine. Most of the miners were younger. A few were older, much older. Stryker guessed those men were either making one last try, or maybe they'd worked the mines so long, they didn't know what else to do. The young ones had the eager look of optimism. The older ones had that wrung out of them years ago. They looked old–and worn. Their rugged hands, curved from years around a pick handle. Regardless, both young and old, held to the belief that they might get rich. Few did. Stryker studied their faces; he was glad he wasn't a miner.

Another fifteen minutes passed and the train whistle blew. The car couplers clanked as the locomotive began pulling out of the station. There weren't conversations with anybody on this trip. Even the young ones knew enough to not aggravate the oldsters with annoying questions.

His ribs hurt when he moved, but they hurt when he didn't move, too. The pills... *to hell with the pills. No telling what kind of condition Morgan might be in. She could be in pain too.* However, it was beginning to sound as if Morgan had come to Grass Valley willingly. *Anyway, if she's hurting, I will too. I'll feel better when I find her.*

Out the window, Stryker saw walls of heavily forested evergreen trees, yellow pine, red fir forest pine, and lodgepole pine. Then he saw deciduous trees, scrub oak, and canyon oak with bay laurel filling in the spaces nearer to the ground. Forty minutes later, as the train drew closer to the mining area, many of the larger pine trees near the tracks had been cut. They were squared off and used as support beams in the mine shafts, Stryker figured. Oxen teams farther away on distant hills, where there was still good timber, pulled logs on skid rows down to railroad tracks. Skid monkeys (boys) ran in front greasing logs with animal fat. Farther away, steam donkeys winching logs to the skid roads blasted puffs of steam out of their smokestacks.

Stryker heard thunderous booming ahead, even above the noisy Baldwin locomotive. He'd been around mining towns and knew the sound. Stamp mills, wooden two-story buildings, came into view, lots of them. Mills crushing the ore made a thunderous racket and in Grass Valley, they worked twenty-four a day, seven days a week, three hundred and sixty-four days a year. Miners took one day off a year to celebrate Miners Day.

The train slowed as it passed the massive workings of the Empire Mine. On the hills above, Stryker saw tunnel openings where ore carts began their ride on tracked rails down to the stamp mills. At the far end of the valley, four-man tents sat in neat rows to house the miners. Most miners labored in the tunnels. Others pushed ore carts to the stamp mills. Still, more men rolled logs off the flatcars and hauled them in wagons to the sawmills. The Empire mining operation was huge. The mine would have 367 miles of tunnel shafts by the time it shut down in 1956.

All this was for producing gold. Men died getting it out of the ground and more died after it got dug up. Rich folks even made jewelry toilet seats with it. *Taking a shit while seated on gold must sweeten the smell.* Ahead, a logging train rolled onto a side rail to dump logs.

Stryker got off the train with the miners and walked back to take the roan down the cattle ramp. The ground shook beneath his boots from the constant pounding of the stamp mills. The Empire Mine wasn't the only mine around Grass Valley. There were the North Star Mine, which was second only to the Empire in production, and the Golden Treasure Mine, Larimer Mine, Granite Hill Mine, Gold Hill Mine, Peabody Mine, Crown Point Mine, New Eureka Mine, Spring Hill Mine, Conlon Mine, Alpha Mine, Saint John Mine, the Scotia Mine, and many more. Over 250 stamp mills, each one with up to 80 stamps, pounded ore. It was a noisy place. The constant booming shook the low-hanging clouds or seemed to, anyway.

Heavy morning cloud cover blotted the sun. It was the kind of morning where drizzling rain could happen at any moment. Higher up, the tops of hills were shrouded in the mist. However, today's weather wouldn't bother miners digging in the tunnels.

Stryker climbed onto the roan and rode toward the mine manager's office, a two-story building having a block foundation and outside walls made of fortified stone. It still hurt like hell to lift his arms and pull himself onto the saddle. He pushed harder with his stirrup leg. That helped, the pain was becoming like an old friend, and in a way it connected him to Morgan. He didn't question how that worked. It just felt like it.

In addition to the manager's office, the stamp mill, a warehouse, blacksmith shop, machine shop, hoist house, assay office, and other sundry buildings were constructed on the five-acre mine site with block and stone. A donkey engine cable pulled ore carts on steel rails. The rails ran from the hoist house and down into the mine shaft. The carts were also used to bring men in and out of the mine. The mine itself was a diagonal shaft with horizontal drifts, sprouting from the main tunnel at 100-foot intervals. In later years, the shaft was an incredible 11,000 feet long and reached a depth of over 5,000 feet beneath the surface.

An all-black buggy with shiny fancy brass workings was parked in front of the mining office. Stryker dismounted, hitched the roan next to the buggy, and entered the building.

The first floor had four separate work rooms for supervisory work staff. The upstairs housed offices of the mine owner and manager's offices, and three other rooms with map boards of the mine. The maps were on large rectangular tables that stood waist-high and had no chairs around them. Stryker saw a door with a sign which read "Mine Owner." He opened the door and walked in. A massive mahogany desk dominated the room. A nattily dressed man sat behind the desk in a large high-back, leather chair. Three other men sat in smaller leather chairs in front of the desk.

"You Bourn, the owner?" Stryker asked. He stepped closer.

I'm Bourn, Jr., but I just sold the mine." Bourn sat behind the desk. He had on a brown tweed jacket with green velvet lapels. "So, if you're looking for work, you'll have to ask the new owner." William Bourn, Jr. was around thirty-one years old and had taken over running the mine in 1879. William Bourn, Sr. had accidentally shot himself in the stomach and died in 1874. William Jr. had spent a few years in Europe before returning home to run the mine. He updated mining operations and sold out in 1887. His cousin, George Starr took over as superintendent in 1887. Starr began working as a mucker in 1881 and rose in ranks quickly. The man was widely recognized as a mining genius.

"Not looking for work," Stryker replied.

"What are you looking for?" Another man asked. He wore a tweed jacket and sat in a leather chair facing the desk. He then swiveled around to Stryker.

"Take that up with the owner. Where is he?" Stryker was about to get unpleasant.

"I'm Jim Hague," the man in a tweed coat, turned and spoke. "I own the mine now." James Hague was a portly man in his fifties, sporting a white handlebar mustache with a beard.

"You brought a woman from San Francisco in the past few days. Where is she?"

"What the hell are you talking about?" Hague eyed the Peacemaker and followed that up with, "My wife is in San Francisco now. She's visiting there. Doesn't like the mining business." Hague was a well-educated Harvard graduate. A businessman and not all that handy with firearms. He decided along with the rest of the men to not ask Stryker about the stitches.

"I brought my girlfriend from San Francisco recently. What of it?" asked one of the two men in denim and khakis seated in front of the desk.

He appeared to be the only man by the stove who worked in the mines. He was in good shape with rough, strong-looking hands. One could tell he was trying to be assertive but Stryker's fierce features and the Colt on his hip were a hinderance.

"Your girlfriend," Stryker growled. "Who are you?"

"George Starr, I'm superintendent here." George remained seated.

"Where is she?" Stryker didn't like what he was hearing.

"Grass Valley, but she'll be going back to San Francisco in a few days. What do you want with her?"

"Message from Senator Hearst." Stryker turned on his heel and headed for the door without answering. He neglected to ask the woman's name on purpose. Pushing Starr into a confrontation would serve no good purpose. He could find out the girlfriend's name in town. Killing Starr now would have caused problems and caused a delay. He mounted the roan. *What the hell? His girlfriend?* He had to admit the other reason he didn't ask her name; he didn't want to hear him say the girlfriend's name was Morgan. He couldn't blame Morgan if it *were* her. Starr was a successful miner. Starr and Morgan would have that in common, and what did Stryker have to offer Morgan? A romp in the bedroom every few months wouldn't keep a woman satisfied, no matter how good the romp. Regardless, Stryker decided, he'd find Starr's girlfriend—*girlfriend, shit!*—and at least make sure she is Morgan, and unharmed. *Besides, if she stays with me, the damn jinx will kill her.* Stryker dug his heels into the roan's flanks.

The ride to Grass Valley from the Empire Mine was a little over a mile. It gave Stryker time for reflection. The mining town had grown to over three-thousand in population and he would have to ask around to find Starr's girlfriend. What would he do if the woman is Morgan? What would she do?

If she's only staying a few days in town, probably meant she would be in a hotel, Stryker reasoned. He'd locate the best hotel in Grass Valley and start there. Twenty minutes later, Stryker entered the town from the east. He rode along Colfax Avenue until he came to Mill Street and turned north. Most of the houses were tightly packed and hastily built wooden structures. More substantial dwellings were constructed with stone. However, a few stately Victorian mansions owned by the wealthy were also wooden. Business buildings like the Grass Valley Bank, the library, and the schoolhouse was more solidly built. You could say, Grass Valley was a typical mining town, but this one had the potential to be more. Many mining towns in the west were on bare, rocky hillsides or on barren landscapes that were difficult to get to. Grass Valley was aptly named, being in a fertile green valley.

About halfway up the street, after passing three saloons, a general store, a restaurant, a tailor shop, and a boarding house, Stryker reined roan in front of a barbershop. An old-timer, perhaps waiting for his turn, sat on a ladder-back wooden chair in front of the shop. He was smoking a pipe and reading a newspaper. On second thought, the old man in over-alls, a dirty white shirt, and a felt bowler hat wasn't waiting for a haircut. He and the hat had been around, and he could be just sitting on the chair, passing life. Stryker leaned forward and rested his forearms on the saddle horn.

"Where's the best hotel in Grass Valley?" Stryker had no idea if Starr's girlfriend would be staying at upscale lodging. He knew Morgan would be, though. He'd start with that. Morgan used to say the best was good enough for her.

The oldster on the chair looked up from his paper. He started to say a smart-ass reply and then saw Stryker's face, cut wound and all. "That'd be the Holbrooke House, mister. Head on up Mill Street there to the end and look left. You'll see it." He then raised the paper in front of his face.

Stryker reined the roan leftward and prodded its flanks. The Holbrooke House on Main Street is a two-story brick building painted white with green trim around the windows and doors. A balcony ran along the front of the second story for guests to sit and watch street activity below. With only twenty-eight guestrooms, each room was sumptuously appointed nonetheless. The Holbrooke stood as first-class lodging in town. *If Morgan were staying in town, she'd be there*, Stryker reasoned. He hitched the roan and stepped onto the low stoop to a door with a glass upper half. "Holbrooke Hotel" was etched in the glass. He opened the door to rugged luxury. Dark mahogany wood, stone masonry on the walls, leather sofas and chairs to sit in while waiting to check in, and Persian rugs over smoothly planed oak floors in the lobby were impressive. Not anywhere near the Palace, but it would be good enough for Morgan. *If the best is good enough for her, what's she doing with me?*

"Got a message from George Starr to give his girlfriend," Stryker said to the clerk who stood behind the polished mahogany desk. Stryker patted his shirt pocket. "Know George Starr?"

"Everyone knows George," the young man said. He was smartly dressed in a short-waisted, brown suede jacket, a white ruffled shirt, and gray wool slacks, said with a toothy grin. "She's having breakfast in the dining room." He extended an open palm toward the Golden Gate Saloon which also functioned as the hotel's restaurant for fine dining.

Stryker spun on his heels to see where the clerk pointed. An open arched entrance presented the saloon and eatery. More dark rich wood on the walls, marble table tops, leather chairs by the tables, and simple elegance adjacent to the marble-topped saloon bar. He quickly stepped to the dining room. There she was, sitting with her back to him. Dark ash brown hair, shoulder-length, thin body—*Shit, it is her.*

"Morgan." Stryker coming up from behind her, spoke softly. She didn't hear him. He gently tapped her shoulder. "Morgan." He raged inside.

"Excuse me." She twisted about to look at Stryker, holding an empty fork.

She wasn't Morgan.

"Who are you asking for?" She was pretty with gorgeous blue eyes. Her face was perhaps a little too round, but she had a nice friendly smile.

"Thought you were someone else." Stryker felt an urge to hug her for not being Morgan. He was immensely relieved. *Shouldn't be,* he chided himself. Morgan's still missing, and in danger. He straightened and turned to leave.

"Sorry. Does Morgan look like me?"

Stryker stopped dead, turned, and said, "From the back, yes. Any other women like you staying here?" It was a long shot now.

"Not that I know of." Her smile faded a bit. "Maybe she's working as a..."

"She's a mining engineer."

"I'm Francine." She eyed his stitches briefly before drifting to the pale eyes. "You might look for her in Nevada City. It's about five miles north of Grass Valley. Some of the wealthy stay up there to get away from the mill pounding," Francine offered a nervous smile. "Is she pretty?"

"Yes." *Maybe I should thank this woman.* "Like you."

"I hope you find her." The smile brightened.

Stryker swung about and walked from the restaurant.

Francine watched Stryker as he stopped and spoke briefly with the desk clerk before leaving the hotel. She stared pensively at the front door for a moment, and then turned and stuck her fork in the scrambled eggs.

Now what. Stryker stood outside the hotel, before stepping down to the street. He looked up and down Main Street. No reason really. He surely wouldn't find Morgan walking on Main Street in Grass Valley, but he was at a loss. He thought Morgan had come to Grass Valley. It seemed like a good lead. He'd almost wanted her to be here. Now, he realized that wasn't true. More than finding out she might have betrayed Hearst or more than learning she might have left him, Morgan had integrity. Principles, the woman stood on a high mountain of principles. It would have been disappointing to learn she wasn't that person. Stryker drew a deep breath; Morgan hadn't fallen off the pedestal. He stepped off the stoop and onto the street. After unhitching the roan and climbing into the saddle, feeling the damn rib pain, Stryker reined the horse north on Main Street figuring he'd catch the road to Nevada City. He could have ridden back to the train station and asked about the Nevada City train, but it was before noon and it should only be a half-hour's ride, even an easy one. The road ran alongside the rails.

It was a half hour, but not all that easy. The road between the two mining towns lay rough and rocky at times, causing the roan to stumble, jarring the ribs, which in turn produced grunted curses. About halfway there, the train passed him.

Stryker rode across Deer Creek and entered town at the bottom of a hill. Nevada City, like Grass Valley, grew up on low-rising slopes, protected by ridgetops and promontories. Nevada City had a population that only reached a fourth of Grass Valley's. It did at one time have a population of ten thousand. Only about four thousand lived there when Stryker rode into town. However, it still had an ample number of saloons, hardware stores, stables, restaurants, banks, and hotels, the best of which was the National Exchange Hotel. Churches had sprung up as well and began introducing righteous morality. Of course, there were plenty of prostitutes who served to lighten miner's pockets as well as their testicles. The town even has a monument commemorating the ladies of the evening.[i]

The town had miners, merchants, gamblers, two doctors, three lawyers, and a couple of preachers. Stryker passed some of these folks as he rode up Broad Street. None paid him much attention. Saloons, stores, eateries, and other buildings, stretched up the hill. Individual homes collared both sides of Broad Street top of the hill and there the street curved around a corner.

The first building to his left was the National Exchange Hotel, or as some called it, the National Hotel, and he swung the roan to a stop in front. A large rectangular brick building, the National faced Broad Street with a balcony on the second level. Due to several fires in the past, the town citizens chose to finally rebuild with more fire-retardant material. Stryker tied the roan off to a hitching rail by the entrance doors. A slight breeze sprung up, rustling shrub oak leaves behind him. He spun in a low crouch with his Colt drawn and hammer cocked.

"A little jumpy, aren't ya?"

Stryker swung the Colt, aiming it at an old timer ten steps away who was sitting on the far side of another hitch rail with his back against the hotel holding a half-empty whiskey bottle in his lap. Stryker, a little miffed he hadn't seen him before, mumbled out loud, "Must be getting old." He'd been keeping an eye on the street while he hitched the roan. Still, the mixed breed chided himself for the slip.

"You keep up on news in town, or do you just sit around and get drunk?" Stryker eased the hammer forward and slipped the Peacemaker back in its holster.

"Keep to myself mostly. Stay outta people's way. Better for my health. I hear a thing or two now and then." The fellow had long scraggly hair and a beard which was either tobacco stained or just plain filthy. He was thin in face and body. The oldster could have been anywhere from thirty to sixty. Hard to tell on a man who lives in the bottle. He struggled to his feet, holding the bottle out while he dusted off his rear end. "Think I'll get outta your way, now."

"Seen a new woman in town? One with dark hair, early thirties, attractive?" Stryker asked in interrogatives, currying favor with the old timer.

"Ain't seen none that I know of." The old timer remained standing in place. He took a swallow from the bottle and wiped his mouth. "Why?"

"She might have come here on her own, or maybe kidnapped."

"Kidnapped."

Stryker sensed the old man had more to add. His hand flashed to the Peacemaker and pulled it. "Tell me about kidnappings."

"I jus' heard rumors."

"Tell me."

"There's a house down near Deer Creek, southwest of town. It's a two-story house 'bout halfway 'tween town and the Mountaineer Mine. I hear it's a whore house."

"Enough, 'I heard' shit." Stryker cocked the Peacemaker. "No one's gonna miss you."

"It's a brothel. I been there. Used to work the Mountaineer 'fore this." The old man lifted the bottle. "All the miners visited them girls. They keep 'em locked in rooms. Ain't sure how they end up there. That's all I know."

"How I find it?"

"You can follow Champion Mine Road for 'bout a half mile west of town, then cut south to Deer Creek. Or you can just follow a feint trail by Deer Creek to it. The creek runs west for a bit, then turns southwest. The mine and whorehouse are south of the creek." The old man added, "Got a red lantern in front." He moved back a couple of steps. "Mind if I go now?"

Stryker hooked his boot in the stirrup and swung on to the roan. A pained grunt was his reply. He headed back down the hill to the creek and turned west on the creek trail.

The drunk watched Stryker as he rode out of sight. He then let out a huge breath and took a long drink from the bottle.

The trail ran feint like the old man said. Stryker figured most mine traffic took the road, however following the creek trail sounded shorter. Sure, the whorehouse was another long shot, but might be worth it. He tried not to think of Morgan being locked in a room and forced to fuck filthy miners but he couldn't help it. He girded the roan into a quicker pace. Thorn bushes grew heavily along the trail as it wound along the creek, pricking the roan's legs, drawing small drops of blood in its tough hide. A few thorns got through Stryker's denims to prick his knees as well and Stryker began to have second thoughts about taking the trail. The roan would probably agree. The stream provided a water source for vegetation to grow thickly, almost obliterating the path. In years past, the creek was worked to pan for gold, but nowadays mining took place underground and the creek trail was no longer used. Shrub oak and pines grew thick on the hills as well, making it difficult for Stryker to see the trail ahead. Finally, he came to a well-traveled road that ran perpendicular to the creek. He took it to be out of the heavy brush, and thorns. That road intersected with the mine road from town and he took it heading southwest. It was then he realized the road would have been shorter and quicker. *Fuck.* On the way back, he'd take the road.

In two hundred yards, Stryker came to a wooden bridge over the stream. After crossing the stream, he looked up and saw a two-story house sitting up on a hill. Must be it, he figured. No other buildings were in sight, and this was the well-used road to that house. The lantern was not lit. Regardless, it had to be the brothel. The lantern probably burned at night. He rode up to the house and dismounted.

A buckboard painted a pale green with two horses sat parked in front of the house. On the second floor, a balcony with a white wooden railing ran the width of the front. Stryker hitched the roan to a rail near the wagon and climbed the two steps to the front door. It was a single-door, painted bright red. A wooden sign on the right side of the door read, *"Welcome Miners."* The lantern was hung on a metal hook next to the sign. Stryker thought about ripping the damn sign off the wall, but he gripped the brass doorknob and opened the door instead.

It was nothing like the bordellos in San Francisco, at least the ones he'd seen anyway. It was not necessarily bare bones in the living room, which functioned as the business office, but it was not overly furnished either. Lit kerosene lanterns hung on the walls. Two more sat on a pine desk by the back wall. A matching pine swivel chair was behind the desk. Brown flowered wallpaper covered the walls. A door in the rear probably led to a hallway, a stairway to the second floor, and perhaps to a kitchen, was shut. A steel safe, chest high, stood behind the desk and chair. The safe had a spin dial combination lock and handle. Stryker glanced at the safe and wondered how much money was in it. Against the wall opposite the desk was a couch covered with a white quilt. The quilt, soiled in spots, had a big red rose embroidered on it. The couch sagged in the middle. Three men and a woman were in the room. One man sat in the swivel chair behind the desk, another sat in front of the desk with the woman, and the third fellow rushed up to Stryker. He carried a gun, a holstered Colt .45. All four people eyed Stryker, looking none too friendly.

"What can we do for you," the doorman asked. His greeting dripped in sarcasm. Stryker didn't like sarcastic toughs. *Smart mouth assholes.* Interactions with them almost always became contentious. Since Stryker is still alive, one can reasonably assume how they turned out. The greeter was stout rather than tall. Muscular with a menacing scowl, Stryker guessed he'd pitched a few miners out the door, and he appeared to be sizing up the mixed breed.

"Looking for a woman."

"We got plenty of them here," the man behind the desk spouted, adding to the sarcasm. Then a bit more welcoming, he continued, "My name's Cable. I own the place. This here's Mary and Cecil." Cable pointed at the two seated across the desk. And over there is Bruce." Have a seat on the sofa and we'll bring one out for ya'."

Stryker figured Bruce kept the peace. Mary worked with the prostitutes. He wasn't sure what purpose Cecil had. Procurement maybe. Mary too, perhaps.

"Bring 'em all out." Stryker stepped deeper into the room.

The doorman raised a hand to push against Stryker's chest. "Now just a minute, mister! You ain't ordering nobody around here."

Stryker parried the arm and blasted a heel hand to the doorman's face. His nose bloodied, his eyes watered, and Bruce went for the Colt.

Stryker was quicker. The Peacemaker was cocked and at the man's belly before the Colt made it out of the holster.

"Easy, gentlemen!" Cable shouted. "No need for any of that. "Bruce, stand aside and let mister… what's your name, sir?"

"Stryker."

"… Stryker be welcomed here. Now, Stryker, instead of bringing the ladies downstairs, Cecil will escort you up to the rooms, and you can choose a girl. Prices vary. Pay first."

Cecil stood but he remained next to his chair, unsure what to do.

Mary had twisted around in her chair to study Stryker, and then she got out of her chair too.

Mary, dressed in a frilly red dress, with the top dropped down showing her meaty shoulders, might have once occupied a room upstairs. However, the pounds had outpaced the years. She had a stern expression, facial rosacea, and bloodshot watery eyes; she had the appearance of a drinker. If Mary were available for sex, she would probably not be his first choice, unless the beer goggles were really thick.

"Come with me," Cecil finally growled, with no hint of a smile. He shuffled to the hallway door. Stryker holstered the .44 and went with him. Bruce's hate-filled watery eyes followed Stryker.

Cecil led him through the door which opened to a hallway and staircase. At the far end of the hall, Stryker saw a dining table and a sink in the kitchen. Cecil clomped up the stairs attached to the left wall. Under the steps, Stryker saw two doors. He saw two more down the right side of the hall. Stryker suspected the rooms were used by Cable and staff. A series of doors ran along the right side of the second floor, and a shorter group of doors extended down the left, beyond the stairs. Stryker noted how closely the doors were spaced apart, suggesting rooms within were small. Each door had a sliding latch so the doors could be locked from the outside. *Rooms or cells?*

They stopped at the first door on the left. Cecil slid the latch open and opened the door for Stryker to look inside. A woman who sat on a single bed gazed up at him. The bed was the only piece of furniture in the small room. There was no window and just four walls with a kerosene lantern on the wall opposite the bed. The woman, appearing to be in her mid-twenties, did not offer a smile. She was very thin. Her hair hung closely cropped just below the ears. She had on a faded blue bathrobe and no shoes. Her face looked pale and she looked up at Stryker with pleading eyes. She wasn't Morgan.

"I want to see more girls," Stryker said. He didn't like what he saw, not because she wasn't Morgan, or that the woman displeased him.

Other rooms, or cells, were much the same. The women, although different ages, sizes, and shapes, expressed similar demeanor.

"What don't you like about 'em?" Cecil sounded irritated.

"Show me all the girls. I'll decide then."

Finally, after three more rooms, and Stryker not making a choice, Cecil groused, "Dammit mister, what the fuck do you want?" There's only four girls left." Then Cecil asked, "You like young? I see, maybe *that's* what you're looking for. Why didn't you say so?"

Cecil led him to the next room. "Twins in here. They might be young enough for ya'," Cecil laughed. He slid open the latch.

Two young girls sat on the bed. Really young girls. Stryker was stunned. "How old are you?" He asked.

"Ten," one replied. They had been in the room long enough so that they no longer cried.

Cecil sensed Stryker's revulsion. "Add 'em together, they're twenty," he joked.

"Show me the last ones," Stryker ordered.

Cecil shrugged his shoulders and walked ahead for the last two rooms. Stryker pulled the razor, moved closer, reached around to lift Cecil's chin and slit his throat. Cecil took two more steps and coughed. Blood spurted from the gash. Gagging on blood filling his severed wind-pipe, Cecil fell to his knees. Holding a hand to his throat, he tried to breathe.

Stryker put a boot between Cecil's shoulders and shoved the dying man to the floor. With bulging eyes and a gaping mouth, Cecil lay on the planked boards, retching blood from a slashed throat.

Stryker wiped the razor on Cecil's shirt and opened latches on the last two rooms. The girls in each appeared to be in their early teens. Too young for the business… and there was still no Morgan. A futile effort. The entire trip had been useless, a huge mistake on his part. On top of that, he faced a delay getting back to San Francisco where he might do some good. If Morgan were to suffer injury or death while he was away, it would be his own fucking fault. His fault for chasing after the wrong clues. His fault because of the god-damned jinx. His fault for not staying away from her. All his fault. *Shit.*

He'd stumbled onto unmitigated evil. One, his code wouldn't let him ignore. Often hard to predict what triggers wrath in the unpredictable mixed breed. It might have been the ten-year-olds, or the imprisoned women, or the men who pissed him off. Who knows. Normally, he steers clear of situations not involving him, but not today. Not this time.

Stryker stepped over Cecil finishing his death gurgle, and walked back to the first prostitute's door. Yes, she was a prostitute, but an unwilling one. He unlatched it and entered the small room. Grabbing the woman by the arm, he lifted her to her feet and led her into the hallway.

"Unlock all the doors and bring the girls into the hall at the top of the stairs. I'll yell for you to come down. What's your name?"

"Loreda." Loreda fidgeted nervously, rubbing her hands together against her chest. "Cable won't like this. He'll hurt us. Hurt us bad." She stifled a scream and pulled away to go back into her room.

Stryker grabbed Loreda again and slapped her face. "Unlock the doors!" He wrenched the woman around and shoved her toward the next door. That's when she saw Cecil's body in a pool of blood.

"Is he dead?" Loreda asked, staring at the bloody carnage.

"Yes. Unlock the damn doors." Stryker watched her unlatch three of them before he turned to head down the stairs.

As he descended the stairs, he pulled the Peacemaker and thumbed back the hammer. He crept along the hallway and cracked open the office door, and then he nudged it wider with the gun barrel before stepping into the room. Bruce stood beside the desk, ten feet away, with his back to Stryker. Mary still sat across the desk from Cable, but Stryker couldn't see him. Bruce blocked his view.

Stryker aimed and fired. The bullet entered the back of Bruce's head, blowing bone and brains out of his left eye. Bruce fell against the desk and then rolled to the floor. Stryker pointed the Peacemaker at Cable.

"Open the safe." Stryker shot Cable in the shoulder and thumbed the hammer again.

"Stop! I'll open it!" Cable leapt out of the chair holding his shoulder. He moved over to the safe and knelt. He wiped his hand on his pants and spun the combination. There was a faint click. Cable turned the handle and opened the safe.

"There. It's open. Now don't shoot again!" Cable stepped away from the open safe.

Stryker shot him in the forehead. Blood splattered the wall behind Cable. He fell back against it and crumpled to the floor, leaving a long red streak down the wallpaper.

"Mary, take the money out and count it."

Mary froze, stunned by what she saw, two bodies with exploded heads. Four very big holes. Ten pints is a lot of blood. That's about how much a human body holds, and it looked as if each body drained all ten pints out of its head. Blood carpeted the floor. Mary failed to receive and register Stryker's order.

He slapped her, slapped her hard. "Get the money from the safe. All of it." Stryker drew back his hand again.

The slap brought Mary to life. She raised both hands in front of her face, palms out to ward off another blow.

Stryker grabbed Mary's dress in front, pulled her over Bruce's body, then gave her a hard shove. She yelped, slipping in the blood, but stayed on her feet by grasping the safe's open door. Blood flooded around it and she bent down to retrieve the money instead of kneeling.

Stryker watched her pull out the cash and stack it on the desk. It took several trips wading in the blood. She arranged the money in even piles and began to count. It took some time. There were a few one-hundreds with the rest of the cash in twenties, tens, fives, and ones. She laid the hundred-dollar bills in a separate pile. When finished, she looked up at Stryker.

"Forty-four thousand, and ten dollars."

"Make ten piles of four-thousand each.

"You're giving each girl four thousand?" Mary asked with a puzzled frown.

"They earned it."

'What about me?"

Stryker shot Mary in the chest, left center. The shock came and went on her face. She collapsed to the floor. Her body shuddered twice, and then she died.

Cable and his cohorts spent the last four and a half years kidnapping and holding women and girls as sex slaves. A few had even died during that time. The miners never complained. The price for sex was cheap. Local authorities got freebies so they never interfered. Everything went along swimmingly until Stryker came along. If there is such a thing as bad karma, Cable and the gang built a mountain of it. Then one day, karma arrived for payback. Stryker was the paymaster. The mixed breed wandered in and what he saw, revulsed him. He killed without emotion, had no prior planning, and would have no regret. An efficient killer. He had long since stopped having self-recriminations. He simply eliminated the lives of those who crossed him. None got a second chance. One could say the four he just killed had done him no physical harm, and that would be true. However, they had assaulted his senses and his code of morality. Slapped him in the face with it. None of them knew of their offense and were not cognizant of the insult, but that did not matter. Although just before death, a hint of why Stryker killed them might have crossed their minds, well maybe not Cecil's. Stryker didn't care if they knew why he shot them. No sermons. He eliminated them. That was that.

"Loreda! Bring 'em down!" Stryker swept the one-dollar bills off the desk and stuffed them in his shirt pocket.

Stryker heard the women coming down the stairs, stepping cautiously on the creaking boards. He waited patiently. Finally, he saw Loreda's head peaking in the room.

"Have the women come in," Stryker ordered. Understanding their reluctance, he added, "They're all dead."

Loreda saw the bodies and called out behind her, "C'mon girls. It's all right."

Stryker stood by the desk. The girls saw the bodies first, then him, and then the money. They crowded around, careful to stand away from the bodies and out of the blood. One girl kicked Cable in the face. Payback. It was a hardy blow. Then she joined the rest of the females, staring at the money.

"One pile for each of you," Stryker said. Loreda, you and someone you can trust ensure the young ones keep their share. I'll ride with you to Grass Valley. Clean up and buy new clothes there. Take the buckboard out front. Pick up the money and stuff it where people can't see it. Leave now. Get in the wagon. Wait for me to come out."

"Come grab the money, one apiece, and let's get outta here," Loreda shouted. They each grabbed a stack of bills off the desk and shoved one another rushing out the door. "Get in the wagon." Loreda pushed the last girl out of the office and came back to Stryker. "What are you going to do?"

"Go now," Stryker ordered.

Loreda ran out. None of the girls had taken the spring bench, so she climbed up on it. "One of you girls, come here and sit with me." Loreda patted the bench beside her, and a young teen scrambled next to her.

"Let's go!" Shouted a girl in the wagon.

"He said to wait for him," Loreda yelled back. The girls got to their knees and crowded to the side of the wagon closest to the house. They stared at the door. None talked while several minutes passed.

"Who is he?" One girl finally asked.

"I don't know," Loreda replied.

"He killed all those bastards?"

"Yes, and watch the damn door!" Loreda got anxious while waiting for Stryker.

Inside the house, Stryker removed lanterns from the walls and hurled them down the hallway, bursting the glass globes and spreading the flames. He took the two lanterns off the desk and smashed them against the back wall. After watching the fire get a good start, he walked out of the house. Flames grew rapidly and soon burst out the front door. He led the roan and the wagon horses away from the house. Stryker and the girls waited as the two-story building burst into a raging inferno. The house was set in a clearing. Maybe the fire wouldn't spread to the surrounding trees. It's doubtful if any of the eleven people watching worried about it. The four inside didn't give a shit.

After more than a half hour, Stryker climbed on the saddle. "Let's go." He pulled the reins and headed the roan down the road. *Four assholes. Too bad they don't issue hunting permits for assholes.* Stryker would most certainly get his limit during hunting season (year-round for him). He bagged four today. He might have mounted them in his den with the others. He could proudly point at a truly magnificent asshole and boast, "I bagged this one in northern California."

Stryker doesn't have a den.

"Get up!" Loreda snapped reins and pulled them left to follow Stryker.

Stryker stayed on the road and led the girls back toward Nevada City until they came to the Grass Valley junction, where he turned south. He rode twenty yards ahead and never once offered conversation. The girls also remained silent, each perhaps involved with her own predicaments.

Forty minutes later, they entered Grass Valley forty and dark clouds rolled in and it started to sprinkle. He took them onto North Main Street and then on Mill Street in the center of town. They stopped in front of Russell's General Store a quarter of the way down the street. They arrived at Maxine's Clothing and Accessories Store. A handprinted sign in the window read, "Featuring the New Rational Dress Line."

"Take them in Russell's. Buy toiletries and traveling cases, and then go to Maxine's for new clothes. After that, put 'em on a train to St Louis. Take care of the young ones."

The rain fell harder when the girls scrambled from the buckboard and dashed into the store.

Stryker rode away toward the train station. He was finished with the girls. Any more from him and people might call him a do-gooder, and the mixed breed is no-gooder. He turned up the collar under his Stetson. He wondered briefly if the four bodies in the whorehouse got properly cooked before the rain doused the fire.

Rain slanted down in sheets, pelting his face. He hunched forward and tipped his head down to shield his eyes. Late in the day and with the rain's help, day turned to night. *Shit, no train at the station.* Stryker dismounted and quickly stepped across the wet platform to the ticket window. The ticket agent wore a green visor and was busy making entries in a ledger. The badge on his shirt pocket read, "Roger." Roger looked up at Stryker. "You Stryker, mister?"

"Yes." Bad news coming, Stryker figured.

"Got a telegram for ya'." Roger slipped a yellow envelope under the iron bars to Stryker. His name was written on the envelope.

Stryker stuffed the envelope in his jacket pocket and hurried into the station. It was empty. He brushed the rainwater off his jacket front and pushed back the hat. It didn't help much, but at least the rainwater wouldn't drip on the telegram. He dried his hands by crossing his arms and drying his hands on his shirt under the jacket. Instead of sitting on a bench, he stood by a wall lantern before tearing open the envelope. The telegram was folded in half. He opened it and read the typed words on the yellow paper.

"Stryker. Received ransom letter for Morgan. Come back immediately. George."

Stryker put the telegram back in its envelope, stuffed it in his pocket, and went to the ticket window. "Ticket to San Francisco."

"Figured you'd want a ticket to somewhere," Roger said, shaking his head. "Sorry, mister. The train ain't goin' nowhere tonight, nor for the next two or three days. The bridge washed out over Bear River. A whole section is gone. You can't even walk across it."

Stryker slammed his fist on the counter. "I need to ford the river." The startled clerk jumped back.

"Ain't no good place." Roger edged up to the ticket window. "The Bear's a torrent of raging flood water now. Overflowed its banks. A three-day storm up north caused it. We're getting some of it here in Grass Valley today." The clerk leaned forward, placed his arms on the counter, and added, "Mister Stryker, that river's washin' down trees, limbs, mud, rocks, dead animals, you name it. It can't be crossed. I would be suicide. Bridges up and downstream are gone too. The telegraph is still up though. That's how I know 'bout the river. Listen, even if you rode the thirty miles, and it'd take thirty miles to go around, other streams are now swollen rivers, between here and Colfax or to Sacramento if you're headin' that way. The mines are shuttin' down too, flooded 'em. Saloons, restaurants, stores, hotels, and whore houses, reckon they'll all be open for business. I'd get a room first." Roger turned away from the window, leaving Stryker to deal with the bad news.

"Shit." Stryker strode over to look out the door. He'd seldom seen rain coming down this hard. No reason to doubt the ticket agent. He went back to the ticket window. "Want a telegram sent." Stryker waited impatiently for Roger's attention, and added, "To Senator George Hearst, Palace Hotel, San Francisco:"

The ticket agent glanced at Stryker and then continued writing the text. "Delayed in Grass Valley due to floods. Could be two or three days. Want news updates. Stryker"

Roger counted the words using his pencil, and said, "Dollar-fifty, pay first," before looking up. When he did, he saw the pale eyes narrow. "I'll send it first."

Stryker shoved two dollars under the bars and watched as Roger tapped out the telegram.

"Here's fifty-cents back." The ticket agent pushed two coins across the counter. Anything else, Mister Stryker?"

"Need a room."

"Rhenda's boarding house is around the corner. Close to the station, here. She charges four dollars a night and that includes breakfast."

Stryker snugged his jacket collar under the Stetson and stepped out in the pouring rain. Horse and saddle were soaked. He took the reins and led the roan around the station. Even though it was early afternoon, the storm made it eerily dark. He sloshed through the mud, passing Rhenda's boarding house before realizing he had to turn around and go back. The house was set a hundred paces back from the street. He looped the reins around the hitching post. He never liked to use the reins to secure a horse, but he used them tonight. He climbed four steps to the door. Two square columns supporting a center-peaked porch cover provided some respite from the downpour. A crude, handwritten clapboard sign next to the door read, "Rhenda's Boarding House." It was not a very large house, one story, maybe two or three bedrooms. Larger boarding houses closer to the mines housed twenty men or more. This one most likely had an all too typical history, a married couple, maybe with family lived here, and the man died. The widow rented a room or rooms to earn money. Stryker rapped on the door.

Two more times of hard knocking and someone answered. The door edged open. Someone peaked through the crack. A faint light from the interior shadowed a female. He couldn't tell for sure, but the shape of the hair looked like a woman's, and lower down two more heads appeared, a boy and girl.

"Yes?" The woman spoke with hesitation. The door barely stayed open.

"A room," Water dripped from the Stetson as Stryker looked down at the kids. "Roger sent me." He hoped that might open the door wider.

"Roger? My brother?"

"Station clerk, ma'am." Stryker wanted out of the rain. "I need a room for a night or two. You Rhenda?"

"Yes." The door opened a little wider. "What's your name?"

"Stryker. I need shelter for my horse, too."

"There's a shed around back. Knock on the back door when you're ready to come in."

Stryker led the roan around the house to the horse shed. A single-seat privy was forty yards beyond the shed. Built with a back wall, two sides, and an open front, the shed provided limited shelter from the rain. Enough room for three horses, it had a hitching rail and half a bale of straw. A water bucket sat in the corner. Not many horses tonight. Stryker guessed that stood for other nights as well. It could be her first boarder. He took the saddle, blanket, and saddlebags off the roan, and hung them on the rail. After pulling the bit and bridle he put on the halter and looped its straps on the rail. He pumped a bucket of water from the well and sat it by the roan. Throwing the saddlebags over his shoulder, Stryker stepped back into the rain.

It was raining even harder when Stryker sloshed through ankle-deep mud to the back door. She had left it slightly open. He pushed it open wider and stepped into the kitchen. Rhenda and the two children were waiting for him. They stood on the far side of the kitchen table, which was bare except for two schoolbooks and a lit kerosene lantern. The wood-planed table was six feet long and had four straight-backed chairs around it. Rhenda and the children stared at him without speaking. Stryker took two long strides to the table, spun a chair around, draped the saddlebags on it, and sat to pull off the muddy boots. He then rose and placed them by the back door.

"Roger told me four dollars a night," Stryker said.

"Four dollars a night. If that's what Roger told you, then fine."

"Breakfast too." Stryker immediately regretted adding that. Rhenda looked thin, very thin. She had hollow cheeks and dark sunken eyes. He could see her collar bones the outline of boney shoulders underneath the faded gray dress, a garment which had seen better days. One side of her brunette hair was clipped back. The opposite side hung straight and stringy with a few white strands. The boy was maybe twelve years old, and the girl was perhaps in single digits; they were also thin and had almost outgrown their clothing. Haggard hung heavily on Rhenda's features. Stryker thought she wasn't bad looking. "I'll eat breakfast somewhere else."

"How long might you be staying?" Rhenda asked. She put an arm around her son's shoulder.

"A day; could be two or three."

"I'll show you to your room." Rhenda pulled her arm away from the boy, picked up the lantern, and led him from the kitchen.

Stryker followed. The children trailed silently after him. The single-story house had living room space, the kitchen they'd just left, and two bedrooms, one on each side of the living room. A small blaze burned in the brick fireplace near the kitchen door. Furniture was sparse; a couch that sagged in the middle leaned against a side wall, and two covered chairs sat by the fireplace. There was a coffee table in front of the couch. Rhenda showed him to the bedroom. It was on the left of the front entrance. The planked floors lay bare; there were no rugs.

"This will be your room," Rhenda said, swinging the lantern to show two single beds separated by a small desk next to the wall. It was the children's room. "Jamie, Mandy, pick up your things and take them to my room," Rhenda said. The children didn't have much to pick up. A few clothing items. There were no toys.

"Where's the man of the house?" Stryker asked as the children gathered their clothing.

"Killed in the mine three months ago," Rhenda said matter-of-factly.

Stryker dug four gold coins from his pocket. "The first night, here." He took Rhenda's wrist and placed the coins in her hand.

She wound her fingers around the coins and dropped her arm. "C'mon, kids." The boy and girl rushed from the bedroom. Rhenda followed the children, closing the door behind her.

Stryker stared at the two beds for about half a second before he threw open the door. "Rhenda!" He called, coming from the bedroom. "I'll find another place to stay." He started for the kitchen.

"No!" Rhenda grabbed Stryker's arm and pulled it tightly against her body. "Please, you can't leave." It was a desperate whisper.

"I'm not throwing the kids out of their bedroom."

Rhenda tightened her grip. "Kids, go to your bedroom and close the door. She waited until the bedroom door closed. "There's another bedroom."

"Not throwing you out either." Stryker pried Rhenda's hand from his arm. "Keep the four dollars."

She stepped in front of him. "You won't have to."

"Have to what?"

"Throw me out of my room. Stryker, I have a house payment in four days. I've sold the horse, sold the saddle. I clean rooms at the Holbrooke when they call me. It's not enough. The only thing left for me is a bordello, but that would leave Jamie and Mandy alone at night."

"I said keep the four dollars."

"I can almost make the payment if you stay three nights."

"Lady, I…"

"The bed's big enough," Rhenda cut in. "Room for two."

Stryker studied Rhenda's face, determined, pleading. *Damn*. He had twenty-two dollars. Might not be enough to give her twelve and have enough for another hotel room and train fare to Colfax. *Shit.* "All right."

"Thank you." Rhenda launched herself at Stryker, burying her face in his chest, she wrapped her arms around his waist. She didn't cry, tried not to anyway. The woman held tight, though. A little too tight, but at least beneath the sore ribs. His arms hung free. What to do with them? Stand there like an ass? He drew an arm around her and cradled her head, even caressed a little.

"I'm three months behind on the mortgage payment," Rhenda snubbed. She jerked away. Collected herself. "You should get out of those wet clothes. Do you have dry… I would offer… but James wasn't as tall… I should throw his stuff away." Rhenda wiped her nose on her sleeve.

"In my saddlebags, ma'am."

"Use my bedroom to change. There's a wash tub in the kitchen if you want to… I can heat water for it."

A hot bath sounded good to Stryker after being bone-chilled in the rain, but instead... "I'll just change for now."

He gathered up the saddlebags and went to her bedroom to change clothes. Yes, he would bathe before bed. Rhenda kept a clean and neat bedroom. The bed was made and everything was in its place. The woman may have been poor, but he'd noticed the rest of the house was neat and clean too. He stripped off his soaked panhandles as well, and put on dry trousers and shirt with nothing underneath. He only had one set of underwear. Gathering the wet clothes and holding them away from his worn, but clean and dry, dungarees and shirt, he opened the door and stepped into the living room.

"Where can I hang these?"

Rhenda took the clothes and went into the kitchen. He followed. She draped the clothing over the chairs.

Stryker grabbed the panhandles and stuffed them in a boot.

Jamie and Mandy, stood at the kitchen doorway, giggling.

"Jamie, do your homework," Rhenda ordered, pointing at the book on the table.

"Ah, ma," Jamie groused. "It's long division. Can't you help me with it?"

"You'll have to do it on your own."

"I can't. I get stuck."

"I'll look at it," Stryker offered. He knew he was getting close to acting like a decent human being, but he suspected Rhenda had trouble with math. *What the hell?*

"You know arithmetic, Mister Stryker?" Rhenda asked. She appeared surprised, puzzled.

"A little." Stryker was an artilleryman in the Army and worked for a munitions company developing howitzers afterward. There's lots of trigonometry and math in artillery.

Stryker opened the book and removed the paper showing division problems. Jamie had printed definitions for *divisor*, *dividend*, and *quotient* at the top of the page and one example problem under that. The problem to solve had multiple numbers for the divisor and dividend and it was obvious Jamie didn't understand how to carry numbers and remainders.

"Sit here," Stryker ordered, pulling out a chair. Let's work on it. Within a half hour, Jamie was doing more complicated division problems without Stryker's help. The accomplishment as a teacher rang hollow, though. The small measure of success in helping the boy was immediately overshadowed. He thought of Morgan and his frustration of not being able to help her.

Rain stopped pounding on the roof and outside the window, and Stryker watched it turn into a sprinkling. He made a quick decision to ride to the Bear River bridge. He grabbed his wet clothes, including the long johns, and stomped back into the bedroom. Saying nothing when he came out, Stryker walked to the kitchen and picked up his boots. Opening the rear door, he went outside to pull them on.

"Are you leaving?" Rhenda asked, standing in the doorway behind him.

"Depends on the bridge." Stryker put his boots on and faced her. "A woman's been kidnapped in San Francisco. Thought she was brought here. I was wrong. Now, I gotta get back." He spun on his heels and clopped through the mud to the station. The train engine billowed steam and waited in front. Three flat cars loaded with cut logs were hooked behind it.

"News on the bridge?" Stryker asked at the ticket window.

"Been working all night on it. Be a while yet. The river's still rising

"Shit!"

"Yeah, sorry mister. Water's coming from upstream and it'll be at least a day or so before it crests." The ticket agent walked away and then reappeared. "Say, mister. If you want, we're running logs out to the bridge, you can ride out there on one of the cars and back if you want, no charge. Won't do you no good, probably, but you can see for yourself." The agent disappeared again.

The engineer wearing customary overalls and an engineer's cap stood on the platform sipping from a mug of coffee when Stryker approached him. "When you leaving?"

"When I finish my coffee."

"The ticket agent," Stryker hooked a thumb toward the ticket window, "said I could ride to the bridge."

"Go ask the foreman, there." The engineer nodded at a man wearing course denim and a plaid shirt inspecting the stacked logs. "If he says okay, then okay by me." The engineer pointed the mug at the flat cars. "Ride top the logs with the other men so you don't get crushed if they shift." He continued slowly sipping coffee as he watched Stryker climb onto a rail car and scramble to sit with the loggers.

The engineer eventually finished his brew and climbed into the engine cab. Not long afterward, wheels rolled and the Shay locomotive inched forward. The log men eyed Stryker suspiciously, however disapproving comments remained in their throats. None of the loggers wore a .44. Stryker didn't care for the logmen either. Loggers in Felton tried to chop him to death.[ii] So, everyone rode in silence. The loggers didn't even talk among themselves.

It took an hour to reach the bridge, or what was left of it. The train stopped a hundred feet from the river gorge. Stryker and the men climbed down off the logs. *Shit!* He was not pleased with what he saw. Fifty feet of the center section was completely gone, washed away downstream, and the river was a mud-colored maelstrom of rapidly churning flood water. Normally, water ran thirty feet wide in the gorge, depending on where you measured and the time of year. Now it overflowed its banks by an additional twenty yards, flooding down the canyon. In the narrowest sections where the river was constricted by rock walls, waves in the rapids rose thirty feet high. Stryker was awestruck by the water's power. This was not going to be a two or three-day repair. The ticket agent had not exaggerated like Stryker suspected, and he watched impatiently as loggers piked logs from the flatcars. Now, shit, he had to hurry back to Grass Valley and find another way to Colfax. The unloading of the logs took an hour and a half. Fortunately, they'd been bucked, cut to size, and branches cleaned, making the unloading easier. Men waiting at the bridge carried peeling spuds for debarking, the final preparation for the wood used in rebuilding the bridge trestle. A man who appeared authoritative, he wore clean clothes anyway, stood off to the side. He held blueprints under his arm and wore glasses. Stryker approached him.

"How long before you get the bridge repaired?"

"Several months. It'll take a couple of days just to get the logs down here. It'll take a week more to set footings before rebuilding support beams. Then we start throwing on cross beams. You wantin' to cross?" The bridge engineer asked, watching the raging river.

"Yeah, in a hurry."

"Come back in three days. The logs they're peeling are for a raft. Planks coming in the morning. Gotta let the river settle down 'fore we can get a cable and pulley over." The engineer removed his glasses and wiped them with his handkerchief, then went on. "Three days oughta' be 'bout right. It'll still be rough but we'll try using what's left of the bridge and ropes to secure the raft."

"I'll be back," Stryker said, and he headed over to the train. With unloading completed, Stryker joined the loggers who were climbing back onto the flatcar. A few minutes later, the locomotive began gathering steam and the engineer backed the train to Grass Valley.

The Shay engine took another hour on the return trip. The loggers unloaded and hustled to the nearest saloon. Stryker saw the engineer observing men running from the flatcar, and he walked over to him.

"You get the logs farther north," Stryker asked, in a statement of course.

The engineer nodded. "Up past Nevada City, towards Rock Creek. Closest white pines for cutting. Having a hell of a time getting 'em to the rails." Rubbing his chin, he scrunched his face. "Why you askin'?"

"Are creeks and rivers flooded?" Stryker asked the question in an interrogative. He wanted the information.

"One of the reasons we had such a rough time. The whole area north of Grass Valley for several miles is like an island, surrounded by swollen and impassable rivers. We had to haul the logs to the rails by oxen. River's no good." The engineer supplied the information without rancor. He probably figured, *why mess with a man looking none too friendly?* He hurried after his men.

Stryker trudged through the mud and back to Rhenda's. *What to do for three days?* At least the damn rain stopped.

He circled back of the house and after making sure the roan had feed and water, he knocked on the door. There was no answer, so he knocked again, louder. One of the children yelled from inside. He couldn't tell if it was the boy or the girl. Could have been either one. Still nothing. Stryker was about to walk away when the doorknob turned and the door cracked open. Upon seeing Stryker Rhenda opened it wider. She had a purple towel wrapped around her and soapy water dripped from her arms and legs. Her hair was drawn up on top of her head, held by a thin green ribbon. Soap suds were on the bony shoulders too. *Damn, woman.* Stryker was highly vulnerable to bony shoulders and patellae. It was a weakness.

"Come back for your horse?" Rhenda didn't move to invite him in.

"If it's all right, I'll stay three days."

"I was taking a bath."

"I can come back later." Stryker swung to hop off the porch.

"No, come in. I'll get dressed." She hurried from the kitchen, leaving wet footprints on the floor. The tracks grew fainter going to the living room and on toward the bedroom. Soap suds bubbled in the washtub by the stove.

Stryker drew up a chair and pulled off his boots. Shadows stretched over the kitchen floor from the waning sunlight through the window. He glanced outside and guessed there was slightly over an hour of daylight left. There was no sight of the kids. Staying out of sight, good. He hadn't expected kids. The mixed breed was not especially fond of children. Little noisy mortgages. That's how he saw them. Rhenda returned to the kitchen.

"You hungry?" Rhenda wore a gray wool skirt and a white cotton blouse. Her hair lay combed and pinned back on one side, like he'd first see her.

"Been a while since I ate."

"Join us for dinner then." Rhenda went to the cabinet and pulled out four porcelain plates. "It'll be ready in about an hour. Beans and potatoes." She then lit the wood-burning stove and set two pots of water on top. Two almost-empty burlap sacks lay on a side table near the stove, one labeled "Beans" and the other marked "Potatoes." Rhenda poured four cups of beans into one pot and dropped four potatoes in the other. "Takes a while to boil 'em."

"Where's the children?"

"In their room. I told them not to bother you."

Stryker hadn't realized his displeasure with kids, especially those not his seed, was so noticeable. Ordinarily, he wouldn't give a shit, but now that didn't entirely sit well with him. Sure, he wanted to be careful about becoming a possible stepfather. He'd chided himself for helping the boy with math. That's what a father does. However, Rhenda had picked up on his loathing of children. Truthfully he would probably be the same even if they were his. Stryker wasn't cut out to be paternal. He'd read how a male lion will sometimes kill and eat his own cubs. Regardless, Stryker would never be a family man, much less a good one. Might have been different when he was younger. Perhaps with Leigh. Who knows. Now though, he did feel a slight regret that the children knew he didn't care for them. *Better they know now, rather than having a bigger disappointment later,* he told himself. *And trying to explain why wouldn't do any good either. So there, that's the way it is.*

"They're building a ferry raft at the river. Should be ready take me across in three days."

Rhenda said nothing. She picked up a piece of wood and added it to the stove fire. She stirred the pots with the wooden spoon.

"Gonna exercise the horse. Back in a bit." Stryker pulled on his boots and left. Outside, he went to the roan, grabbed the halter, and led the horse around the house and away from town. The roan followed dutifully behind.

Sure, he could go back and act differently for three days. Play nice to the woman and kids. No, he couldn't. It wasn't in him. What good would it do? Matters would be worse when he left, and he wasn't about to give Rhenda money and sleep in a stable. Why sacrifice for a misfortune not of his making? The Stetson wasn't white. After walking a half hour on the road leading out of town, he headed back. He decided he'd be himself, answer questions with short replies, pay his rent, and leave in three days, even if the raft wasn't ready. A fair trade, nothing more, nothing less.

"The children took their baths while you were gone," Rhenda said, opening the door for him. "I put fresh water in the washtub. It's still warm, I'm sure. Soap and towel on the table." She marched from the kitchen.

Stryker knew without Rhenda telling him, she had gone to the children's room. It was dark outside and a lit kerosene lamp on the kitchen table gave only flickering light. He undressed. The water had remained warm. He settled into the tub to soak. The warm water felt good on his sore ribs and he waited a bit before washing. He suspected Rhenda wasn't having him take a bath for his benefit, and it surely wasn't for her benefit. Instead, he figured she preferred the bed not to be soiled. He couldn't blame her. He had just about finished cleansing himself when Rhenda returned. She carried a man's nightshirt and a towel.

"You can wear this." Rhenda draped the nightshirt over a chair. "Here." She tossed him the towel and walked out.

Stryker wondered what to put on after the bath, the clothing he'd just taken off or his long johns, neither of which were dry. Rhenda solved the problem. Although the nightshirt was probably short, it would nevertheless cover up the important parts. He rose from the tub, used the towel, and dried himself. He sat to dry his feet, knowing he would get no more kitchen visits. Afterward, he donned the nightshirt. It was short and he looked silly in it. *Shit! Was her husband a midget?* It didn't even reach his knees.

It may have been an hour, maybe even two, that Stryker sat at the kitchen table. He dozed on and off. Rhenda was either in the kid's bedroom or her own. She could be wondering if he planned to sleep in the kitchen. Eventually, he'd go to her bedroom and climb into bed. He just felt damned awkward. Rhenda might not even be in it. Finally, Stryker realized he had put it off long enough. He got to his feet, blew out the lantern, and after waiting a few minutes for his eyes to adjust, made his way to her bedroom.

A candle burned on the nightstand by his side of the bed. Rhenda lay curled away from the light. Stryker stepped to where the bedding was turned down for him.

"I thought you left," Rhenda said softly.

"Thought about it."

"You look like you're wearing a dress in that nightshirt."

Stryker blew out the candle and took off the silly nightshirt. He crawled between the sheets, staying close to the edge of the bed. Sleep wouldn't come easily. He lay awake for the better part of an hour. Rhenda's quiet breathing told him she wasn't asleep either.

"Stryker, I need four more dollars."

He said nothing.

"My house is worth three hundred. I owe sixty-two. If I don't catch-up the payments by Friday, I'll lose it."

Stryker kept his back to her, keeping quiet. He was trying to figure out how much more money he could spare. Maybe he could let her have four more, he calculated. He was about to tell that when Rhenda spoke again.

"I'll earn it."

What did she mean by that? "How?"

"You can have me."

"I'll give it to you, Rhenda." He started to turn over. His ribs crunched and he groaned.

"You hurt?"

"Ribs."

"What happened to 'em?"

"Got jumped in San Jose. Got most of my money."

"Oh." She paused, perhaps wondering how many men it would take to rob him. "I don't want charity, Stryker."

"My ribs, Rhenda. It's no good." They didn't hurt that badly. Stryker might have toughed it out, but he wasn't going to let her earn it like that. It would ruin it, anyway.

"I'll get on top."

More than just four dollars? It has been a while for her.

Rhenda scooted closer. Moving gingerly, she lifted off the covers and straddled his thighs. She surprised him by having nothing on. Touching lightly with her tender hands, it didn't take long for a response. Rhenda rose to her knees and scooted forward. Then she eased down, slowly, getting used to his size.

She took him in completely and began a slow grind. Leaning down and placing her hands on his shoulders she raised until only the tip remained inside. Then Rhenda did something no other woman had done before. She tightened the lips of her vagina around the head of his penis and began moving up and down–slowly. *Didn't know a woman could do that... shit! That feels good. How'd she learn this?*

Damn woman! You're making it hard to hold back. He grabbed her hips and lifted her off until the urge to come subsided. Her hips were soft, yet firm and that didn't help. Getting a firmer grip on her hips, he shoved her down on him. He put his finger between her legs and began caressing a very swollen clitoris. It took a bit, but then he felt her thighs trembling and knew she was getting close. Rhenda's face was close to his; her mouth by his ear, and he felt her breath growing rapidly. A quiet little groan grew from deep inside, rose to her lips, and slipped in his ear. Her body shook for several seconds and then relaxed.

What the hell? Why waste this? Rhenda and Stryker enjoyed each other's company for the better part of an hour. When finished, she used her talented vagina to lift off him without making a mess. She left the bed and returned a few minutes later with a warm wash cloth. After cleansing him, she curled up close.

"Would it hurt your ribs if I lay my head on you?"

"On my shoulder."

She nestled in close to his ear. "Stay with me."

His silence told her he would not. If she had seen how tightly his eyelids were squeezed, she would have known he wanted to. A lot of emotion crowded into the bedroom. Its dust settled heavily on them. Stryker caressed the back of her neck and her hair. Then a little before midnight, they fell asleep.

Which would a woman prefer, a goody-two-shoes who never strayed, or a man who did once, maybe twice, and still chose her?

The next night during dinner, Rhenda announced the children needed to get more rest and she ushered them to bed early. The children needed more sleep the following night as well.

Stryker traveled to and from the bridge for the next three days. By the third day, the ferry raft was ready for trial runs and the foreman told him to prepare for a ride across the river the next day. He said the roan would have to go alone with only the helmsman. Stryker would go ahead and then wait for the horse on the second trip.

Stryker broke his self-imposed rule of not helping Jamie with math. In the mixed breed's private code, he felt he owed Rhenda additional compensation... *what the hell*? He was human and so was Rhenda. When he said goodbye, there was no hugging, no kissing, or anything close to that. Their time had ended.

Two weeks after Stryker's departure, Mark Cleary, the banker from Colfax visited Rhenda. He told her he had a buyer for her house. At first, Rhenda declined the offer, but when he revealed the dollar amount, she changed her mind. The price paid was twenty-five hundred dollars. A new house in Sacramento had been set aside for her if she wanted it. It cost four hundred dollars and was in a good neighborhood near a school. She was offered a job working for the Governor if she was inclined.

"I don't know who you're friends are," Cleary said. "But they must be mighty powerful."

"I had no idea," Rhenda muttered.

CHAPTER SIX

Stryker and the roan finally made it across Bear River. He had more control over traveling to San Francisco. Three days in Grass Valley had benefits, maybe costly benefits. The delay was frustrating, and the time with Rhenda added more guilt. What if something had happened to Morgan? Something he could have prevented had he been in the city? What if that damn jinx cost Morgan's life, losing her life because she got too close, or due to his failure to save her? These ruminations ran through his mind on the way to Colfax. When the roan slowed, he dug in his heels.

It took most of the day to reach Colfax, not because of the ride to the ferry, nor the ride from the river to town. Stryker had not expected the long line of other people waiting to cross. He should have known. *Shit!* It soaked up three long hours. He was tempted to jump the line, but he didn't.

The sun hovered above the western hills by the time Stryker rode into Colfax. A train headed east waited at the station. It was the wrong direction. The ticket master told him the west-bound Central Pacific wouldn't arrive until ten o'clock that night. It was enough time to see Mark Cleary at the Cookeville Bank before it closed and pick up the two hundred dollars. He hurried to the bank and returned to the station to buy tickets to San Francisco. Having nothing to eat since breakfast at Rhenda's, he went looking for dinner.

The sun had disappeared and the half-moon had yet to appear; however, newly installed gas lampposts provided enough light to see restaurant names on the far side of Main Street. He picked out three choices, a Mexican restaurant that only said "Mexican Food" on the sign, The Soup Kitchen, and Karcher's Eats. Stryker stepped over the tracks and walked to Karcher's. He entered and looked around at the crowded tables, an indication he'd made a good choice. Two tables sat empty. Menus were handwritten on foot-high parchment papers attached to wooden plaques nailed on three walls, right, left, and rear. Glass-enclosed wax candles sat on each table. Stryker strode to a two-person table by the back wall near the kitchen door. It was probably why it hadn't been taken.

The veal stew with cornbread at the bottom of the menu sounded tasty. He ordered it with a beer. The food came shortly, and he thought maybe he should have ordered something that would have taken more time to prepare. The train wasn't scheduled to arrive for three more hours. Regardless, the stew tasted good, and he ate slowly.

As he finished up his bowl an argument broke out across the room. A large fellow in a brown suit sat with a woman and another couple. Apparently, instead of veal medallions, pork medallions were served to his lady friend. Since the woman ate part of the pork before realizing it wasn't veal, the waitress insisted the man pay for the pork before replacing it with the veal. The discussion was vitriolic. Insults were liber-ally thrown. Eventually, the waitress screamed, "The stupid woman should have known she didn't have veal before eating half of it." That earned her a slap across the face from the man. *Defending his woman's honor,* Stryker figured. The smack drew blood and the waitress, a pretty little thing, cried and ran to the kitchen. Karcher, the owner, came out and the men fought.

Stryker quietly watched as finished his cornbread and stew. He wasn't getting involved. He'd already done too much "do-good'n" on this trip. *His dog, the one not in the fight, sat aside, gnawing on a bone.* His priority was finding Morgan and he'd been delayed enough. Stryker finished his meal, downed the beer, put two dollars on the table, and left the restaurant.

Outside, a gentle breeze brushed his face, chilled by the night air. It felt good. The summer had been long and hot. Fall made him melancholy. Things died in the fall, and for some strange reason, he liked that. He inhaled deeply and continued up Main Street at a leisurely pace. In roughly a quarter mile, the street curved right and ended at Grass Valley Road. Grass Valley, it made him think of Rhenda and her children. She'd lost her spouse, too, and now she struggled to provide for herself and the children. At least *he* had no child burden to care for. *Burden, would that have been so bad? A son or daughter?* If something had happened to Morgan, would he go back to Grass Valley? Stryker gazed down the dirt road. The harvest moon cast a pale light on the road splitting the pines in the distance. No, he would not take that road. He turned and headed back down Main Street to the train depot, where he waited for the ten o'clock train.

The Central Pacific rolled in to Colfax on time. Stryker boarded the train and took his usual seat in the half empty coach. Seats near him in the rear remained empty. When looking out the window, he saw his own reflection in the glass. Nothing for him to read. Coach lanterns were turned low anyway. Train wheels clacked their monotonous rhythm. Other riders sat slumped against each other or against a wall in slumber with their backs to him. After a good bit, Stryker's eyelids grew heavy too. He napped on and off until the train pulled into Sacramento three hours later. Stops in Auburn, Loomis, Rockville, and other small towns along the tracks, briefly interrupted passenger naps. People got on and off quietly. Most of the time, new ones boarded and the coach was filled by the time they arrived in the state capital.

Stryker reached San Jose before daylight and had a two-hour wait before he boarded the Southern Pacific to San Francisco. He unloaded the roan and tethered it by the station before verifying tickets for the remainder of the trip. A station attendant busily sifted through travel bags in the baggage bin, separating pieces to take off the train. Half of the passengers got off the Central Pacific in San Jose as well. All but three went inside the station to wait for the next train. A man and two females, one his wife, and the other woman, older, her mother. They picked up their luggage and hurriedly crossed the platform, then stepped off the planks to go around the station.

Just for the hell of it.

Stryker went around the other side and walked to the back of the station. It was not yet dawn, but it was light enough for Stryker to see three shadows standing in the far corner. All three faced away from him. One peeked around the corner.

Well now, here was unfinished business. Stryker snatched the razor from his rear pocket. Creeping along the rear wall, Stryker clasped a hand over Amos's mouth and sank the razor's tip in his neck under the left ear. The sharp blade sliced smoothly the other ear. Stryker eased him to the ground with blood gushing from the hideous wound. Windpipe severed, Amos coughed twice and lay still.

"Shut up, Amos!" Nate hissed.

Stryker closed behind Rico, put a hand over his mouth, and ran the dripping razor across his throat. Stryker released him and he fell without a whimper.

"Here they come!" Nate whispered over his shoulder. He ignored the sound of Rico's body crumpling to the ground and focused on the three people coming around the corner. Nate leaped out. "Hands up! All of you!"

Stryker didn't cover Nate's mouth. Instead, he cupped the man's chin, lifted it, and used the razor a third time. Nate fell at the traveler's feet, spewing blood, gasping for air. Stryker kicked him in the face.

The three muggers died, too eager to rob their next victims. They should have been more watchful. Death crept behind with a razor and slit their throats.

The older woman screamed. The man wrapped an arm around her. The younger woman, who was very pretty, stood rooted in place, staring at Stryker.

"What do you want?" the man asked. He reached for his wife, but she brushed off his arm.

"Go on. You saw nothing." Stryker leaned down and wiped the razor on Nate's shirt.

"Aren't you gonna cut my throat, too?" The wife asked.

Stryker straightened.

"Here," she said, lifting her chin and running a finger across her throat.

"What's your name?" Stryker asked the husband still clutching his mother-in-law. Stryker wondered who was protecting who.

'Bellamy, Bellamy Brookfield."

"Bellamy Brookfield, this woman your wife?"

"Yes."

Take her home, tie her up, and ram it up her ass. She'll be grateful." With that, Stryker left the three travelers and was near the front of the station when he heard the wife yell out.

"Will you do it to me, mister?"

"Shut up Roberta! For Christ's sake!" Brookfield barked.

"Don't talk to me that way!"

"It's time he did!" Her mother snipped.

The man and women kept at it until Stryker rounded the corner and couldn't hear them.

Stryker went into the station and walked to the schedule board on the wall. It had names of the towns with times displayed using removable wooden numbers. The Southern Pacific train to San Francisco was due in at *7:05 a.m.* He had forty minutes. It was crowded inside. A group of men and women gathered around the metal coffee urn on a table. Stryker hoped it wasn't empty as he wove through the crowd. He took a mug off the table and turned the pot handle for coffee. Only a half cup came out and it poured from the bottom. Fine with him. He liked it strong. A few coffee grounds in the mug didn't bother him. He took the mug and after picking up a discarded section of newspaper, found an empty seat away from everybody to read and sip the brew. He'd almost finished reading the last news item when a tow-headed boy in his teens burst through the station door.

"There's been killin's! Out back! Three men with throats cut!" The boy shouted. He stopped to catch his breath. "Blood everywhere!"

The ticket agent burst from the office, still holding a pencil. He grabbed the kid by the shoulders. "Show me!" He spun the boy around, pushed him toward the station door, yelling, "Someone bring a lantern!" The two dashed outside. Six men scrambled after them, seven including Stryker, who walked out.

It was starting to turn gray outside, but there was enough light to see blood look red instead of black. The men and boy slowly rounded the station with Stryker trailing behind. They got out back and surrounded the dead men. Stryker wryly noticed they hadn't gone anywhere.

"Probably men have been holding folks up," the clerk mumbled, eying the bodies. "Son, go get the sheriff. I'll get something to cover 'em. The train'll be here any minute. You men go back inside." Two men lingered for a moment, looking at the carnage, then caught up with the others. A few minutes later, the ticket clerk came in the office through a rear door. Stryker had seen it in the back of the building and suspected it led to the office.

Men who had gone out to see the killings recounted what they'd seen to those interested, and of course, that was everyone in the station. Separate groups of men and women gathered around to hear the gory details. The tales were embellished a bit, but not by much. No need to exaggerate. Stryker thought it odd, no one speculated about the killer or killers. However, he failed to notice a man describing the death scene while nodding at Stryker, who quietly sat reading the paper.

Off in the distance, a train whistle blew.

Stryker secured his customary seat on the rear bench. A man and woman with twin babies sat across from him. Another man wearing a brown tweed suit took the seat next to him. Right away the babies took to wailing. *Shit!* The parents ignored them. Stryker thought about male lions eating cubs. He did not suffer babies well. The train covered the forty-mile distance to San Francisco in just over two hours and the screamers eventually wore themselves out halfway there. Stryker spent much of the time gazing out the window and trying to figure out a way to rescue Morgan. He arrived in San Francisco with no plan.

CHAPTER SEVEN

Stryker stabled the roan and took a cable car to the Palace Hotel. The entire *damn* trip to Grass Valley was a bust. The early afternoon was dark with heavy rain. *Welcome back to San Francisco. Fitting*, Stryker thought. Sometimes it seemed to him that the city by the bay was *in* the bay. Of course, a welcoming wind blew the rain into the cable car. He jumped off before the car completely stopped. Taking quick strides to the hotel, he entered through the front door and hurried to the front desk, dripping water on the marble floor. Hotel guests gave him a clear path to the reception desk. The opulence of the Palace was often lost on Stryker and especially today.

"Tell Hearst I'm here." The clerks recognized Stryker and knew anytime he walked in, the Senator would want to see him right away. They also sensed he wasn't in a good mood and said nothing about the dripping rainwater.

"Mister Stryker to see you, sir." The hotel attaché said. He was sharply dressed in a maroon jacket with gray slacks and made the announcement in the speaking tube piped to Senator Hearst's room. The attaché waited patiently for a reply. Stryker heard the senator in the tube and hurried off as the clerk said, "You may proceed to room *801*, sir." He glanced at the attaché next to him, and called after Stryker, "Welcome back to the Palace, Mister Stryker."

Stryker ignored the welcome and weaved through the guests to the rising room. The elevator door opened and Stryker entered before the last person exited the car. Only five guests got on with him. Eight other guests waited for another car. After a few uncertain moments, the elevator operator shut the gate and the lift rose. The uniformed attendant called out the floors, stopping on each level. Finally, he called out the eighth floor and Stryker stepped onto the lush green carpet. At the end of the hall, the door to *801* was already open and Stryker entered to find Hearst standing by the eight-foot conference table.

"Here is the ransom note," the Senator said, extending the folded parchment to Stryker. He ignored Stryker's dripping.

"How much?" Stryker asked, grabbing the note.

"No money. Read the note."

Stryker unfolded the paper and read it. *"Miss Morgan will be returned to you unharmed when you have run daily front-page articles in the San Francisco Examiner continuously for a full month, extolling Marxism."*

"Shit!"

"Yes," Hearst agreed. "Sit down over there," Hearst said, pointing to two maroon wingbacks by the bay window. "Let's talk about it."

The two men sat. No cognac, no whiskey, merely a fresh pot of black coffee and two mugs. No fancy porcelain either. Hearst poured coffee for both.

"As you can see, there's no information telling me how to communicate with whoever sent the ransom. I suppose they expect me to give my answer in the paper."

"When did you get it?"

"Three days ago. I had hoped you'd return sooner."

"Got here as fast as I could."

"Figured that. In the meantime, I made inquiries. The most likely source of the demand comes from a radical political group. My friend at the college, Edward Holden, the president, told me about the violent demonstrations they've been having at the school. When I showed him the ransom note, he thought it might be related. The demands are similar. Marxist shit."

"What else?" Stryker asked. "What's been placed in the paper?"

"Nothing so far."

"Put nothing in it for now. Maybe they'll think you didn't get the note. Wait at least week or until you get another note. Give me time to find out what I can."

"University of California, the new college," Stryker said under his breath, not looking at Hearst and gazing out the window.

Hearst heard him, anyway. "Yes, that's the one."

"I wanna talk with the president."

"When?"

"Now."

"I'll send for him. My wife, Phoebe has given the school a hefty sum of my money. He'll come," Hearst grunted. "I expect three hours at the most. What's your room number?"

"Don't know."

Hearst rose and strode to the rubberized speaking tube located on the wall. He placed the pipe cone by his mouth and said, "Senator Hearst, here." He put the tube to his ear for the rely then spoke into the cone again, "Stryker's room number." After getting the number, he thanked the front desk attaché and hung up the tube.

"*812*," Hearst said to Stryker who had gotten up to stand by the conference table.

"I'll clean up. Send for me when Holden gets here." Stryker headed for the door. The reserved room was his regular room with a king-size bed, dark masculine furniture, rich forest green carpeting, and pale green wallpaper. Some day he would have to thank Hearst, but not today.

Could be, Stryker was the only man to get away with giving instructions or orders to the Senator, at least in San Francisco. It was probably different in Washington, but Hearst knew Stryker was good with the gun and blade, and it didn't take much for him to use them. "I'll let you know when he arrives."

When Stryker opened the door to *812*, he found a package wrapped in paper and string lying on the bed. He tore open the wrappings to find a new set of clothing for him, denim jeans, a white cotton shirt, undergarments, and socks. Morgan had started instructing an attaché to make sure he had clean clothing whenever he came to the hotel. Most likely paid by Hearst. She told Stryker he needed to get the trail dust and horse smell off him. Her thoughtfulness hit him. The little things. He drew in a long breath. *Ah damn.* He glanced at the bathroom door and took off his clothes.

All guest rooms in the Palace had full baths; it was one of few hotels to have such accommodations in the country. Stryker ran hot water in the bathtub and got in it to soap himself. There had been times when Morgan walked in and surprised him. He glanced at the door, and for a moment he hoped and then cursed out loud at himself for being stupid. *I need to get my ass out of this tub and find her.* Stryker quickened his bathing, rose from the soapy water, dried off, and got dressed.

Rather than wait in the room with nothing to do, he went downstairs and bought a newspaper. He returned with the *San Francisco Examiner* and looked at the front page first. Even that reminded him of Morgan. Being in San Francisco brought her closer, made her absence more painful, and made finding her more urgent.

In less than the three allotted hours, Stryker heard rapping on the door. He rose from the bed and opened it.

"Sir, Senator Hearst sent me to get you," The smartly dressed young hotel attaché announced crisply. "He's in room…"

Stryker brushed the young man aside and rushed past him.

"I guess he knows the number," the attaché grumbled, watching Stryker hurry down the hall.

The door to *801* hung open and Stryker entered without knocking. Edward Holden had a medium build and height, full head of hair, and a beard, both snow white. He sat at the table with Hearst. Holden sported a bright yellow, purple-dotted bowtie peeking out from under the white cascade of facial hair. Bowties being worth ten IQ points, it probably fit. Another man, in a police uniform, sat with his back to the door. Stryker figured Hearst contacted the police. Stryker had no intention to work with them. Police had to play by the rules. Stryker suspected they had already been there several minutes. None of them rose when he walked in the room.

"Stryker!" Hearst bellowed. "Stryker, this is Doctor Edward Holden, President University of California, and I've asked the police commissioner, Bruce McGee, to meet with us too."

"Stryker," Holden said, good to see you again."

"You know him?" Hearst asked with surprise on his face.

"We were at West Point together," Holden replied, nodding to Hearst as he spoke.[i]

"You went to West Point? Both of you?" McGee asked.

"Yes," Hearst said. "Both are West Point graduates. Please sit down, Stryker."

The commissioner turned in the seat to greet Stryker but remained seated. He was a stout man, barrel-chested with a full head of red hair, a robust beard, and piercing green eyes beneath bushy eyebrows. His craggy rugged face and set jaw said he was a no-bullshit policeman. He gave Stryker a nod.

Stryker went behind Hearst seated at the table's end, and sat next to Holden. A blast of wind blew rain hard against the window and the four men looked briefly at the glass.

"Blowing hard tonight," Hearst said. "Edward, tell Stryker your idea."

President Holden glanced around at each man, drew a deep breath, and began. "We think the woman's kidnapping and unrest at the university may be related, Stryker. If we could find who's behind the protest demonstrations, he, or them, may lead us to who's holding her. Maybe they can be persuaded to halt the violence on campus. George tells me you can be persuasive, Stryker."

"What about police?" Stryker eyed the commissioner.

"We'll continue with our work, investigations, following leads when we get them." McGee looked at Hearst and added, "We'll be available." He appeared none too happy about the arrangement.

"There is more, Stryker." Holden interrupted glaring between Stryker and McGee. "My history professor, Orville Whitaker, has taken quite ill. He won't be able to teach his class for at least a week, maybe two." He eyed Hearst, then back to Stryker. "Would you be willing to teach the class?" Before Stryker could answer, Holden quickly went on. "Teach and work undercover. I think there may be teaching staff sympathizing with the protests. I'm not happy about it, but academic freedom and all that… Stryker, I want you to find out who might be involved."

"And Stryker," Hearst added. "Someone, student or an associate, may know something about Morgan. We have no other clues of where she might be. The clues or tips we've had so far have not been fruitful."

"Will you do it?" Holden asked.

"Get me Tooonug, Paiute Indian, in southern Utah. I need him here in two days."

Holden and McGee gave Hearst puzzled looks.

Hearst in turn stared at Stryker. "Done." The senator had no idea why he wanted Tooonug or where to find him, other than southern Utah, but if Stryker wanted Tooonug, the senator would find him and bring him to San Francisco. Years ago, Stryker and Tooonug had been combatants, then by chance, favors were exchanged, and the Paiute became indebted to the mixed breed. Stryker can be persuasive, true enough. Tooonug can and has been more persuasive. Stryker kills quickly and efficiently. Tooonug has killed many times as well, only not as quickly. Victims were sometimes… messed up. He could extract information from the most recalcitrant interviewees. A Tooonug technique used in the past was to have two participants for interrogation. He interviewed (tortured) the toughest one in front of the other until the he died a painful death. Not surprisingly, the surviving observer was more willing to divulge information. Yes, Tooonug could be useful.

"You look like one of the protesters. No need to cut your hair or shave," Holden supplied, smiling. "Come to North Hall on the campus tomorrow at eight in the morning. Your lectures will be in that building. I'll introduce you to other instructors and staff. No one will know who you really are. I think that's best for now. If you encounter a cool reception, it's okay. Some of the students might like that. Maybe use it to establish rapport and meet outside of class. You'll be on your own, Stryker. In emergencies, get a note to me, say it's about the class. I'll drop by the classroom. I do that sometimes. Don't come to my office," Holden cautioned. "If we meet, it's got to look normal."

"I need the syllabus, textbooks, lecture notes," Stryker said. *If there is an emergency, a note to Holden is silly,* Stryker thought. Academicians are so far removed from reality; they think conferences and committees can handle every situation. He would take care of emergencies his way.

Stryker's request made a favorable impression on the University President. He grinned. "I'll get those materials from Orville tonight and have them for you tomorrow. The class is American History, basic curriculum. I'm sure you can handle it." It was doubtful if Holden really believed that. However, his tone was not condescending. Perhaps the scholar had the good sense not to rile Stryker.

A college professor, who would have thought that, Stryker mused to himself. *Have to learn how to comport myself–act the part, lofty, aloof, and snobbish. Shit, and wear a damn suit.* "I'll see you in the morning," Stryker said to Holden. He pushed back his chair and glanced at the commissioner. After giving Hearst a short nod, Stryker left the room.

"You think he can pull it off?" McGee asked. "I don't think he can. He looks too rough around the edges to me."

"I've been surprised at what that man is capable of," Hearst said. "He is a learned man, even though as you say he is a bit rough around the edges. He is motivated to find Morgan, just as I am. And Bruce, if there happens to be, let's say *disturbances,* leave him alone unless he asks for police help. I don't think he will." Hearst gazed absently toward the bay window beyond the conference table. "I wonder what he wants with that Indian."

Stryker walked briskly to the rising room, took it to ground level, and hailed a horse cab in the turn-around. "Take me to a man's clothing store," he told the driver.

The driver, a stately dressed black man wearing coat and tails exited the Palace roundabout and brought Stryker to 152 Kearney Street. The *City of Paris Dry Goods Store was* established by Felix and Emile Verdier from France in 1850. Some of the finest fashions and accouterments, along with silks, laces, Cognacs, wine, and champaign, from Paris filled the store which later relocated to Union Square in 1896. Eventually, the building, re-structured after the 1906 fire, was sold to *Neiman Marcus*. An hour later Stryker emerged from the store wearing a brown tweed suit–and a chocolate brown bowtie. He couldn't go for the yellow polka dots. He opted for no hat, but he looked dapper. *What I won't do to find Morgan.* He carried the boots, hat, denim, and shirt he wore into the shop in a store bag. In the wrapped paper with string, he held another suit, gray with a suitable bowtie. He was feeling academically intelligent already.

Stryker hailed a cab and returned to the Palace. Not stopping at the front desk, he crossed the marble floor to the rising room. Nevertheless, some ribs got elbowed by hotel staff upon seeing Stryker in his new duds. The elevator operator eyed him with inflated eyeballs, then turned his face to the wall as they rose to the eighth floor. Stryker got off the elevator and fortunately, room *812* was nearby. However, as Stryker opened the door to his room, he heard a loud guffaw coming from the elevator operator two floors below. *Why the hell didn't you change back into your denim at the shop, dumbass?*

He walked into the room and glanced into the bathroom where he saw himself in the full-length mirror. He moved closer to get a better look. He hadn't seen himself in the shop mirror. *Ah shit, you look like an ass, Stryker.* "Get used to it," he growled out loud. "I can't leave here in my old clothes and then change at the school. Fuck it." He ripped off the bowtie and stared at the mirror. *I can do without the damn thing. Fuck 'em.*

As he undressed, Stryker considered a western tie but nixed it. He wasn't going to wear a damn tie, period. One thing he would miss wearing though, was the Peacemaker. The .44 wouldn't do on a college professor. Then he remembered he'd need something to carry books and papers, a bag or a satchel to carry books, papers… and a gun. A satisfied grunt escaped his lungs.

The following morning, Stryker went down to the roundabout, hailed a cab to the Ferry House, and took the ferry across the bay to Alameda. From there, he got a horse cab to take him to the University of California in Berkley. He carried the Peacemaker in the *City of Paris* shopping bag. He didn't wear a bowtie.

North Hall and South Hall were constructed in 1873. The two buildings were the first to be built on campus. The rectangular structures, roughly one-hundred and twenty feet wide and eighty feet deep, had rock and mortar outside the first floor with the upper three floors made with brick and mortar. Opposing stone steps in front cascaded to the second floor. Vertical arched windows punctuated the gabled roof top. Most of the classes took place on the second and third floors.

University President Holden met Stryker inside the doors to the second floor of North Hall. Holden said nothing about a missing tie, but he did notice the shopping bag. "Here, use Orville's case." Holden held out a stuffed brown leather carry case with buckled straps on the flap to Stryker. "It has his books and papers for the class in it. Syllabus too. He said to thank you for covering his class for him."

Stryker took the case. He hung the shopping bag handles on his wrist and unbuckled the case straps. Holding the flap open, he pulled the .44 from the bag and put it in the carry case. It was a tight fit.

Holden saw the gun and eyed Stryker. "All right then, I'll take you to your classroom." On the way to the lecture hall, which was on the third floor, he mentioned other professors waited to greet Stryker. North Hall had no rising room. They climbed the stairs. Holden led him down the hallway's wood-paneled walls to room *308* and opened the door. The top half of the door was clear glass. Stryker suspected that was so Holden could check on professors and students without entering the classroom.

Six males and one female waited to meet Stryker. History was a required undergraduate course, the classroom was large. Six steeply tiered rows of desks, eighteen chairs per row faced the lecture podium in a shallow concave formation. The podium stood front center of the four-foot stage. A thirty-foot ceiling allowed the last row of seats ten feet clearance. To a first-time instructor, the room's size could be imposing. Stryker had commanded several hundred troops and given speeches before battle where many would die. One hundred and eight snot-nosed rich kids would not be a problem.

The seven professors.

President Holden presented Stryker to academicians, only mentioning Stryker as his name. He called each instructor by name and title in the introduction. Holden mentioned Stryker "earned his credentials at the West Point Military Academy." No questions concerning the academy curriculum were asked by the seven, although they surely must have been curious. However, Stryker's countenance did not invite the curious to ask about it. No handshakes were exchanged.

Pompous academicians are how the seven struck Stryker. To be fair not all college professors are pompous, only those full of pomposity. Rodney, Walter, and Dilbert wore suits and bowties, Frederick, and Marcus in turtlenecks. Stryker would not remember what name matched the attire. Magnus wore an ascot. That, he would probably remember. *Who the hell names a kid Magnus?* Stryker made a mental note to ask a question in Latin later. He did take a particular note of the woman, though. The way she dressed, that is. No suit, not even close. She wore a white silk shirt with long billowy sleeves, a multi-colored A-line skirt that almost touched the floor, and her red hair flowed past her shoulder blades held in place by a purple crocheted headband. Her soft green eyes appraised Stryker approvingly.

"Stryker will start tomorrow," Holden announced. "I believe..." Holden withdrew a note card and glanced at it. "Yes, tomorrow and the first class is at nine o'clock. Please lend any assistance to him. He's new to the campus here." He flashed a broad smile and nodded at Stryker.

Stryker, for his part, knew he would *fit right in*. "See you in the morning." He spun on his heels and walked from the classroom.

"Mister Stryker does not appear to be a qualified academician," bowtie Dilbert offered after the door closed behind Stryker.

"He does not appear so, of that we could agree, I suppose," Holden supplied, clearing his throat. "However, he is also in the employ of one Senator George Hearst, and we would not have these fine University buildings, or our jobs for that matter if it weren't for his wife Pheobe– and the Senator's money. Let's be nice to him, shall we?"

"What in the world does he do for Hearst?" Magnus exclaimed, incredulously.

"Teach history to him?" Petula giggled.

"I haven't asked. Nor should you."

"Whose office will he use, Orville's?" One of the turtlenecks asked.

"Hmmm, hadn't decided. Orville asked me to not let Stryker use his. I suppose…"

"He can share mine!" Petula popped up with an all-too-bright smile, then quickly toned it down with, "I mean, if nothing else is available."

"President Holden hesitated, studying Petula for a moment. "All right then. Shall we adjourn to the student union for coffee and crumpets?"

Stryker carried the satchel with papers and Peacemaker out of North Hall and to the campus front where he hailed a horse cab to the ferry. Once across the bay, he caught another cab to the San Francisco Library on Bush Street. Inside the library, the bookshelves were thirty feet high, and accessed with ladders and walkways. Stryker sought the librarian's help and she selected three thick volumes for him on "American History." He shared a large rectangular table with a man and two women. They offered friendly glances, as if inviting conversation. He ignored them, dug the syllabus from the satchel, reread it, and opened a book about the Revolutionary War.

Three hours later, Stryker stuffed the syllabus and fourteen pages of notes into the leather case and left the library. He'd spend another two hours going over the notes at the Palace. Riding in the cab to the hotel, Stryker couldn't help feeling he was wasting more time, but what else could he do to find Morgan? *How about if I stop people on the street, put a gun to their heads, and demand to know where the hell she is?* He hissed an exasperated *shit.*

He stopped at the Senator's room and gave him an update on the teaching job. Wasn't much to tell. Hearst invited him to dinner around seven o'clock and Stryker accepted. In the meantime, Stryker spent time in his hotel room studying the notes. It was difficult to concentrate though. Eventually, he shut it down and changed into denim for dinner. *Yeah, denim.* No need to be undercover in the hotel and to be uncomfortable in the damn suit. Complainers could kiss his ass or argue with mister Colt. He was not in a good mood.

Commissioner Bruce McGee joined Hearst and Stryker downstairs in the men's dining hall. Cigar smoke hung heavily in the room. Real men smoked cigars when gathering for business, card games, or to discuss politics. Normally there were no women, so smoking stogies was not only allowed, it was expected. So much smoke drifted about, and wall lamps hung on the walls glowed dimly in smoky halos. The hall was a clamorous den of loud boisterous talking, guffaws over crude jokes, and shouts for wait staff, all made by those lubricated with liquor. The men didn't pay much attention to the man with the Peacemaker on his hip. Many were regulars. They'd seen him before and in the company of the senator.

Lots of dark mahogany wood trim, white tablecloths, and booths that ran along a side wall had curtains to close if needed. Some meetings required discretion. Hearst and McGee sat in one of the booths. They sat opposite one another in the booth. Stryker had not expected McGee. The commissioner eyed Stryker with contempt as he sat on the other side of the table next to Hearst. Stryker figured McGee saw him as competition and wouldn't reveal anything that might be helpful in the search for Morgan. He suspected McGee wanted to find Morgan first, even if it meant only finding her body. Stryker didn't trust him.

"We found Tooonug in Carson City, in prison again," the Commissioner began. "The Paiute got in a knife fight and the other man, a white man, suffered nasty cuts. Your Indian was found guilty of attempted murder," McGee huffed.

Well, Tooonug started the fracas. Never one to back down from a fight, except the time he encountered Stryker one night after he'd seen the mixed breed's skill with the sai. Tooonug had decided not to challenge the man with the evil-looking weapon. A white man insulted Tooonug to his face. It was about his face. Tooonug's fierce countenance is further exacerbated by his unique ugliness. Rumor has it, the birthing squaws who helped with Tooonug's childbirth, slapped the mother. After many wars with Utes, who constantly stole Paiute women, he became an exceptionally good fighter. The Utes never captured Tooonug's mother. At only five-feet two inches, Tooonug was one nasty Indian. McGee told Stryker the Paiute was on a westbound train to San Francisco.

The Commissioner also said he discovered a mastermind was behind the violent demonstrations at the University. Unfortunately, the young protester who supplied that information, died before he could say who it was or where he could be found. Another demonstrator had knifed him.

None of the other radicals divulged information about the mysterious leader after that. McGee eyed Stryker as he spoke. Hearst had probably already been told.

Stryker smelled a lie. It was a safe bet that a mastermind organized the protests. Usually was. McGee had to show Hearst something, assure the Senator the police were doing their job. *But did the protester die before naming who was behind the violence?*

"How about the faculty at the college, Stryker? Learn anything?" Hearst asked.

Before Stryker could answer, a middle-aged waiter wearing a white tuxedo jacket and black satin slacks, appeared carrying Cognac and beer on a silver tray. He placed a brandy glass in front of the Senator and a chilled mug in front of the Commissioner. He poured both libations with aplomb and placed menus on the table.

The waiter turned to Stryker. "Would you like anything to drink, sir?"

"Coffee, black." Then answering Hearst he said, "Not very much." Stryker suddenly questioned whether this whole undercover operation was simply a convenient ruse by McGee to keep him out of the way.

The waiter spun smartly, skillfully slanting the tray to keep the Cognac decanter and empty beer bottle from slipping off the platter, and quickly marched off.

"Let's go over our menus," Hearst said.

Stryker briefly considered mentioning Petula and that she might possibly provide information about the leftist marchers. She struck him as being at least sympathetic to the cause. If he stayed undercover long enough, and got no other leads, he'd try to find out what she knew. He might do that anyway, but since Tooonug was on his way to San Francisco, arrangements needed to be made. Hearst, and certainly McGee, had told him as much as they were going to tell him at dinner.

"What time is Tooonug arriving?" Stryker asked McGee.

"Three-ten tomorrow afternoon."

"Excuse me, George," Stryker called the Senator George for McGee's benefit, and he got up from the table. Normally, he wouldn't have said, "Excuse me" either.

"Aren't you going to have dinner with us?" Hearst asked, looking surprised. "At least wait for your coffee?"

"No." Stryker walked from the dining room and out of the hotel.

A light drizzle and the early makings of thick fog greeted Stryker outside. He hailed a horse cab. "Take me to the Embarcadero."

The California gold rush in 1849 brought tens of thousands to San Francisco. One-third arrived by ship. When gold fever had finally died down, at least 500 ships that had brought them to the city lay mostly abandoned in the harbor. A forest of masts floated in the bay. The city built a sea wall and the waterfront encroached out in the harbor. Around 200 hundred ships were refurbished and returned to sea. The remaining ships either sank where they were or the encroaching waterfront surrounded them. At least 100 ships lied beneath the streets of San Francisco. Land east of the Embarcadero is flat and was the financial district. Only when a person walks from the shore and moves uphill will they find the original shoreline.

The City of Chester ship was rammed by the steamer Oceanic from Asia that year. It sank in six minutes near the yet to be built Golden Gate Bridge which opened forty-nine years later. Stryker did not know about the bridge, nor did he see many of the ships left over in the bay after the 49er gold rush. Most had sunk or had been swallowed by the expanding shoreline. What he did encounter was the overwhelming smell from the fish markets along the wharf. Europeans, particularly Italians, had turned the bay into a mecca for fishing in their small but sea worthy feluccas, boats perfectly suited for rough seas. Feluccas lay docked at the shoreline where fishermen unloaded salmon, flounder, herring, and crabs. Marketmen hawking the catches blared a cacophony of sales pitches along the wharf. The thickening fog carried the sounds and especially the smell of fish within its vapers. And whether raw or cooked, fish stunk up the Embarcadero.

Stryker stepped from the cab at Fisherman's Wharf. Since the gold seekers overtook Embarcadero, there has always been vagrants, beggars, drunkards, and muggers along the walkway. Stryker encountered many of them as he strode northward on Fisherman's Wharf. A few asked for money. Not until he left The Embarcadero, and into a more dimly lit no-name alleyway, did the request for money become more insistent. However, the sudden appearance of the Peacemaker and a click of the hammer caused would-be muggers to fade into the shadows.

Finally, in a narrow dark passageway littered with crates and trash, Stryker found what he was looking for. The sign in the flickering light of the door lantern read, "Rooms to Rent." He rapped on the heavy wooden door buttressed with iron strapping. Nothing. Then he banged on the door with the side of his fist. The door edged open.

"What do you want?" The gravelly, ancient voice came from a face unseen.

I want Morgan, asshole. "A room," Stryker growled.

"Come in." The door creaked wider. The shriveled-up life form with straggly white hair carrying a lantern turned away, and said, "Follow along."

Stryker couldn't decide if the ancient landlord was male or female. Inside the narrow passageway, three doors on each side were five feet apart and one at the end.

"This an opium den?" Stryker got no answer. There was no stench of the drug, however stale body odor overwhelmed the Embarcadero's fish smell. The landlord's shoulders bent, and he listed to one side, shuffling down the hallway to the seventh door. The old, whatever it was, opened the door to the room. As Stryker stepped into the austere, tiny room he managed a closer look at what turned out to be a very old man. Deeply etched, wrinkled face, he could have been at sea for most of his life. Stryker didn't ask. A metal-frame bed with a two-inch mattress and a wooden chair were the total furnishings. A kerosene lamp hung on the wall. The room was no more than five feet by eight feet. Austere, yes, but luxurious for a Paiute who'd lived outdoors most of his life.

"Toilet?"

"Public one, on Embarcadero."

"How much?" Stryker asked, staring at the small room.

"Dollar a night. Five for the week."

"I'll take it for the week." Stryker dug out a five-dollar bill. "It's for someone else. Here. He grabbed the old man's wrist and stuck the five in his hand. He's a Paiute."

"No Indians," the oldster mumbled, shuffling down the hall.

Stryker grabbed the old man's shoulder, spun him around, and slammed him against the wall. The mixed breed got close, real close, grabbed the landlord's throat, and rammed the sai through the old man's rotting teeth. Blood seeped out the corner of his mouth. "You'll make an exception."

The landlord nodded. Stryker released him.

"Come and go; the front door is locked at midnight." The ancient landlord edged down the wall, eager to escape Stryker. He stopped at the next door, opened it, and slipped inside.

Stryker would rent a boat the next day. He went back around to Embarcadero Street and got a cab to the hotel. A small fish restaurant was on Market Street, and he crossed the street for fish and chips. The sole proprietor stood inside the half-door selling fried cod and potato strips. That was it. You stayed outside. It was not his normal fare; however, Stryker liked the way he served the fish with malt vinegar wrapped in a newspaper. He bought a bottle of beer from the bar next door, and carried everything to his hotel room.

Turn-down service was a bedtime treat offered by the Palace Hotel and Stryker had grown to enjoy the luxury. The bed linen and comforter had been partially folded down, lamps lowered, drapes drawn, and pillows fluffed. The least he could do before climbing between the clean sheets was to take a quick bath, although he had bathed earlier in the day. He owed the linen that much. So, he stripped and took another bath. Tired, he slipped between the sheets and tried to sleep. It didn't happen for quite a while. Morgan had bathed with him two months ago. They had soaped each other; she had sat back against his chest, and he cupped her breasts in his hands, helping them float in the suds. *Was that the last time?*

CHAPTER EIGHT

The next morning, Stryker rose before daybreak, which was not difficult to do in the perennially overcast San Francisco. Daylight bides its time arriving in the city by the bay. Sometimes it doesn't show up at all. After completing his toiletries, Stryker donned his professor suit, minus the bowtie, and took one quick look at the lecture notes before stuffing them in the leather case. He stopped in the men's grill for a cup of strong black coffee, then went to the carriage turnabout for a cab to the Ferry House.

Rain had drizzled for hours, and the cobbled-stone streets glistened with moisture. He could have taken the cable car, but this morning he took a horse cab, preferring to keep his fancy teaching duds dry. "An umbrella," he mused out loud to himself. "I need an umbrella," remembering college professors carried umbrellas, even when it was not raining.

"I have an umbrella, sir," the cab driver offered. He was a young man who appeared to be in his early twenties, and a budding businessman, perhaps. "I loan them or sell 'em to passengers if they wanna buy. "Three dollars."

Stryker mulled over if three dollars was worth the price for a short-timer professor, but it was probably raining in Berkeley as well. Ordinarily, he wouldn't use one. He thought women and men with feminine qualities carried them. However, under the present circumstances, he might as well play the part, except for the bowtie. "I'll take one."

The driver reached under his seat, withdrew a black umbrella, and passed it back Stryker. It had a wooden handle and waxed cotton cloth with four metal ribs which were hinged by the handle to collapse the canopy when not in use.

The driver noticed Stryker studying the device and offered, "To raise the umbrella, the hinges have little slide buttons to lock and unlock. You might want to do that before you get out in the rain."

Stryker gave the young man five dollars, two for the cab ride. He left the umbrella collapsed, planning to use it at Berkeley. Upon leaving the cab at the Ferry House, he positioned the umbrella under his upper arm carrying the leather case. The mixed breed did not quite look the part. He needed a bowtie.

The ferry ride to Alameda took thirty-five minutes. There Stryker caught another horse cab for the forty-minute ride to the university campus. The driver dropped him off in front of North Hall. The rain stopped and he kept the umbrella pinned under his arm. So scholarly, Professor Stryker, headed to college.

The classroom was filled when he entered. As usual, in the 1880s, women were seated in the front rows, presumably they said, it was to keep them separate from the men. It could have been professors had their own reasons, though.

Stryker stepped onto the stage, and the talking suddenly died. Students shuffled about in their desks, re-arranged books, laid out papers, and readied themselves for the class lecture. He had not expected women—or girls. Two or three were quite fetching. When he unintendedly glanced their way, they offered shy smiles. *This is the fucking shits.* Stryker had never been in class with females, much less teach them in a class. This was a new wrinkle. He had prepared the lecture to give battle-field anecdotes, intending to vividly describe its brutal violence, men getting their balls blown off, for instance. Now he would have to step around scenes like that, and much more. Women were present. He sat the leather case on the oak table and pulled out his notes. After ensuring they were properly arranged, he carried them to the wooden lectern and placed the papers on its angled surface.

He took one more look around the students, purposely skipping the females, and began.

"My name is Neville Stryker. I will be teaching the first few classes until Professor Whitaker returns from illness." He noticed several students appeared to be writing down his name, including those in the front row.

"I thought it would be fitting to start this class on American History with the birth of the nation–the American Revolutionary War. Then Professor Stryker continued with illuminating facts and details of America's fight to gain independence.

He told the class about Robert Morris who financed the war out of his own pocket. Morris, born in Liverpool, England came to America in his teens. He established himself in merchant shipping and went on to became the richest man in the new country. When General George Washington was unable to persuade Congress to provide enough funds for the war, Morris used his own money and what he could borrow with his personal backing, to buy supplies and munitions, and pay the troops. Eventually, Robert Morris became bankrupt and went to debtors' prison. He died a pauper.

Stryker told them about Washinton's army. How 231,000 men served but never more than 48,000 at one time. That 28,000 died, 10,000 or more while prisoners of war. On the march to Valley Forge, Washington remarked how the British could easily find his army. All the British had to do was follow the bloody footprints in the snow. The class also learned at Valley Forge, the starving men boiled their leather shoes and boots to eat.

Stryker recounted Nathan Hale's life to the class. Hale, a Yale graduate, was the only volunteer for Washington when the general needed to know the whereabouts of the British as they prepared to invade Manhattan. Nathan was captured and hanged as a spy. Before his death, he wrote two letters, one to his mother and one to a fellow soldier. At all times, Hale comported himself well, acting with bravery. His last words were that he regretted he only had one life to give to his country. Nathan Hale was twenty-one when hanged.

A snicker came from the back row, and Stryker saw the student with a broad grin turn to a classmate and whisper something. The other student, who was looking at Stryker did not share a smile.

Stryker stepped from the stage and climbed up the aisle to where the smiling student sat. He directed a forefinger at the lad and said, "Come with me." The young man rose and followed Stryker down to the front and out the classroom. A few minutes later, he returned with an ashen look on his face. Without saying anything, he took his seat where he had been sitting before, and Stryker stepped back onto the stage to resume his lecture.

Stryker continued with the history lesson for another hour and then dismissed the class. His lecturing finished for the day, Stryker left North Hall and hailed a horse cab to Alameda. After a half-hour wait, he caught the ferry back to San Francisco. He remained at the Ferry House, ate a ham sandwich, and drank coffee while waiting for Tooonug.

Later in the day, University President Edward Holden had a young male student sitting in his office. President Holden's office on the second floor was a spacious fifteen by twenty-foot room with thick brown carpeting. Two oversized windows allowed for spacious views of the campus mall. Cream-colored silk curtains hung by the open windows danced lazily in the breeze. Behind Holden's broad oak desk, volumes of textbooks, encyclopedias, and historical Greek and Western European Philosophical books filled the floor-to-ceiling bookshelves on the three walls.

"He threatened to kill me!" The student seated in one of two horse-hide wingback chairs in front of Holden's desk cried out. The young student bordered on tears.

"What exactly did Professor Stryker say to you, Wilford." Holden laid down his pencil, rested his forearms on the writing pad, and clasped his hands together. Holden's expression displayed grave concern.

"He grabbed me by the neck and slammed me against the wall and told me if I didn't shut my hole and get an "A" in the class, he would find me, no matter where I was, and slit my throat." Wilford absently moved a hand under his chin.

"Well, Mister Wellington," Holden coughed to clear his throat, "Any idea what brought this on?"

"I guess I was a bit unruly, during his lecture on the American Revolutionary War, but that doesn't… do you think he's serious?" Wilford not only looked scared, he was scared. The mixed breed usually wore a fearsome countenance, especially when agitated, and the lad had foolishly trampled upon his bad side. Some might wonder where was his good side?

"I attended West Point with Stryker," Holden told Wilford. "I've also heard rumors about him from Senator Hearst, and from what I know of the man, my advice to you is to remain in class, keep quiet, and try really, really, hard to get an "A.""

Tooonug arrived on the two o'clock train from Reno. Stryker met him when he stepped onto the station platform in the Ferry House. The Paiute wore beaded deerskin shirt and pants, a hunting knife stuck in the band around his waist, and a crumpled top hat he must have picked up somewhere. Maybe he gave the prior owner a close haircut.

"Tooonug, I need your help," Stryker said. He and Tooonug do not shake hands when greeting one another. "A woman has been kidnapped and in danger."

"She, Stryker woman?"

"Yes."

"Tooonug help."

Stryker led Tooonug out of the Ferry House to the horse cabs. They walked down the line until Stryker spotted a driver who was either Hispanic or non-white mix. He figured it better if Tooonug wasn't seen too much. A minority would be more prone to mind his own business.

"Take us to an inexpensive men's clothing store," Stryker told the driver as he and Tooonug climbed in the carriage. Stryker wasn't trying to be frugal. Fancy threads would call more attention to the Paiute than would cheap clothing. Shirt and slacks, maybe a jacket of some sort, shoes, or boots instead of moccasins and the Paiute might pass for Mexican. The cab driver took them to a shabby-looking haberdashery on Turk

Street. The sign above the glass window read *"Nicks Fine Clothing."* Two mannequins were modeling dark dusty suits, one navy, the other black. Stryker turned the brass doorknob and pushed open the weather-beaten, squeaky door.

A short, balding man, wearing a navy-striped suit with pants too long for his stubby legs approached the new customers wearing a measuring tape around his neck. Four wooden tables, eight-feet by four-feet, had large piles of suits, suit jackets, slacks, and shirts thrown together as display merchandise. The store wasn't very large. No effort had been made to separate the clothing by order, other than, perhaps by size.

"You Nick?" Stryker asked.

"No." The old man who was not Nick eyed Tooonug who stood behind Stryker.

Where's Nick?"

"There's no Nick."

"All right whoever you are, I need clothes for this man."

"Sy, Sy Swartz, that's me." Sy Swartz fingered the measuring tape with a nervous hand. "What kind of clothing?"

"Suit clothes, shirt, and bowtie… and shoes." Bowtie, why the hell not, thought Stryker. Goes with the top hat.

"Gotta measure 'im, first. Shoes are in the back." Sy Swartz mumbled, sliding the tape from his neck. He sidled over to the rear of Tooonug, lifted the Paiute's left arm, bent it at the elbow, and stretched the measuring tape from the center of his neck to the wrist. Sy continued the measuring, writing the figures on a small paper pad he kept in a coat pocket. Once finished with sizing, he threw the tape behind his neck and began selecting garments from two tables.

"Try these on. Change rooms in the back."

Tooonug took the clothes. Holding them in his arms, he first stared at the clothing, and then looked at Stryker as if to ask, "What do I do with clothes?"

"Go put them on," Stryker said, nodding toward the rear of the store.

The Paiute marched to the changing room, exaggerating his displeasure by rocking his shoulders left to right, and grumbling, "Tooonug not happy," several times.

A few minutes later, Tooonug emerged from the dressing room, wearing the new clothes, top hat while holding the deerskins in his arms. The clothing fit and he looked like a new Indian—dapper and uncomfortable.

"Shoes," Stryker said, after nodding his approval. He noticed Tooonug stood at least two inches taller than Sy Swartz.

Sy Swartz dropped to one knee by Tooonug and pulled the measuring tape to measure his foot. He pinched the toe end of the moccasin and held the tape by the crease. "Size eight." Then he held the tape across the arch. "Wide." Sy Swartz rose and headed toward the backroom door.

A little while later, he came out with a pair of blunt, square-shaped, black, lace-up shoes. He handed them to Tooonug. Again, Tooonug looked at Stryker. He knew what to do with them this time, but now his countenance displayed anger.

"Just for two, maybe three, days. You'll make a lot of money," Stryker told him.

Tooonug sat on the floor, placed the deerskins beside him. That's when Stryker noticed he wore the belt and knife around his waist. *Shit.* Tooonug took off his moccasins and put on the new shoes, without tying the laces. Sy Swart knelt and tied them.

"How much?" Stryker asked.

"Let me see." Sy Swartz withdrew the paper pad and began penciling the numbers by each article.

Stryker suspected Swartz already knew how much he would charge, and that the figuring was for show, empathizing the number of items.

"Thirty-eight dollars and forty cents." Sy Swartz glanced at Stryker and then added, "No, wait, I forgot the shoes." He used the pencil again. "Forty-four dollars, even. I took off the forty cents."

Stryker knew he was being over-charged. He thought about bashing Sy Swartz over the head with the Peacemaker and giving him twenty dollars. Instead, he said, "We may have to return for more later." He took the money from his pocket and counted out the bills to Sy Swartz. "C'mon, Tooonug." Stryker had forgotten socks, but Tooonug didn't care.

Stryker paid without objecting, thinking that Sy Swartz might not mention anything about Tooonug if asked, because of the possibility for more business.

Outside in front of Nick's Clothing Store, Stryker hailed a cab to take Tooonug to his new rented room by the Embarcadero. Not much talk was made between him and the Paiute. Stryker concerned himself with pondering over whether Tooonug was a good idea, and Morgan–*Where the hell was she? Is she still alive? How much time do I have?* Tooonug sat quietly, staring straight ahead. Stryker had no idea what was running through the Paiute's mind.

On the Embarcadero, Stryker bought baked cod and potatoes for Tooonug, which he hungrily ate with his hands. The Indian did not stand out on the waterfront. All kinds of strange characters strolled the shore-line streets in the 1880s. There were plenty of saloons selling anything from regular whiskey to rotgut, where Shanghaiers with their blackjacks searched for unsuspecting drunkards to kidnap and deliver to ship captains short on sailors. Some bars even had trap doors for depositing drunk men down chutes to waiting kidnappers who would haul them to ships. Many an unfortunate drunk sobered up the next day out at sea. Chinese who brought their opium dens from Chinatown to the back streets of the waterfront trolled for customers who wanted to get high. There were soiled doves to lighten a man's pockets for a rumble in the sheets. Weird characters came from all over the world. So many that one odd-looking Paiute in pinstripe suit, bowtie, and top hat walking down the street next to a foreboding Stryker was not a big deal.

Stryker brought Tooonug to the rented room and left him with twenty dollars in addition to the handful of biscuits purchased on Embarcadero Street. "I'll be back in a while." Was all Stryker said to him. There was no use telling Tooonug to remain in the tiny room. He wouldn't.

It was late afternoon. If the sun were visible, it would be seen dipping into the Pacific. Stryker hurried along Fisherman's Wharf where fishing boats were available for recreational fishermen, or to take a lady for a romantic row along the shoreline–not by the rocky shore but near enough to stay away from ships, ferries, and rough water. The bay can be turbulent at times, especially during high tide entering from the Pacific. Best to stay well within the bay like the boaters rowing kidnapped victims to waiting ship captains. Staying away from rough water allows the Shanghaied a more pleasant boating experience.

Stryker rented a fourteen-foot boat from an old salt who didn't ask questions. He paid the man, climbed into the boat, and took up the oars. He'd rowed before. He pulled away from the dock and began rowing up the shoreline. It brought back memories of Leigh in upstate New York.

They were in a canoe, not a boat, and he paddled the canoe on Mohonk Lake by the Mohonk Mountain Resort. Leigh sat in front of the boat wearing a sleeveless white dress holding a blue parasol to shade her light skin. She smiled and laughed. At times, she let her hand lazily trail along in the water. He remembered it as the best of times. No schedules, no worries–*no body ripped apart and blackened from an exploded artillery shell.*

He gripped the oars tighter and rowed faster. Punishing himself now. It was his carelessness that ended her life. Stryker rowed hard until his arms and legs gave out somewhere past Potrero Point. He slumped forward, exhausted, letting the boat drift. Finally, he took up the oars again and beached the boat in a sandy cove, which would later be called, Warm Water Cove. The cove was relatively isolated, and just south of the California Sugar Refinery that Claus Spreckels built in 1881. Stryker heaved the boat up into the bushes, and away from high tide. Using a piece of driftwood, he smudged out his tracks.

He took a ten-minute walk to the corner of Illinois and 25th Streets and waited for a cab. Not many ran in that part of town and it was thirty more minutes before he heard the horse cab coming down the street. He used the time to sit and think about things, like figuring out how to use Tooonug.

CHAPTER NINE

Back at the Palace Hotel, there was no news yet. Nothing from the commissioner, nor had Hearst learned anything new. No additional contact from the kidnappers. That could be a good thing, giving them more time to find Morgan, or… it could be mean something bad. But neither Stryker or Hearst wanted to consider the bad just yet.

Stryker did not tell Hearst he'd met with Tooonug. That was all for now. Details of how the Paiute might help was best left unsaid, and the senator had the good sense not to ask about it. Like Stryker, he was more concerned about finding Morgan, and if a rule or two got broken to find her.

After the meeting with Hearst, Stryker retired to his room and prepared for the next class. He had a nagging suspicion, the undercover teaching was a waste of time, and he found it difficult to concentrate. He would rather actively engage in bullets, blades, or fists, skills he was accustomed to. Standing in front of students, teaching history seemed unrelated to rescuing Morgan. Still, he couldn't think of anything else to do. Tomorrow, he planned to press Petula and get closer to the woman. He intended to find out if she has any viable information. Stryker did not know that Petula had her own ideas about getting closer.

Protesters greeted faculty, staff, and students as they arrived on campus. Chanting slogans related to Marxist ideology. He didn't know what the protesters wanted, and doubted they knew what they wanted either, other than anarchy. They did not approach him.

Early morning mist gave way to clear skies and the sun shone brightly. Stryker strode past campus buildings and through their shrinking shadows cast on dew-covered grounds.

President Holden met Stryker at the door to North Hall and informed him Petula offered to share her office space. Her teaching schedule did not coincide with Stryker's, but if she met with a student after class, he was to allow them privacy. "Fourth floor, room *412*, I think." Holden pointed a forefinger upward. "Petula sympathizes with the protesters, maybe a little too much. I would have questioned her before now, but then Senator Hearst and I came up with the idea of bringing in someone else." Holden grinned, saying, "You. Good luck. Off I go," and he hurried to the stairway.

Stryker gave Holden time to reach the second floor before he started up the stairs. It was almost time for his class to start. He'd meet with Professor Petula afterward. The Revolutionary War lecture continued with no student snickering. Wilford was especially attentive and took copious notes. Stryker impatiently answered questions from three female students and a male student after class. He still felt odd being called, "Professor Stryker." Walking to Petula's office, he reprimanded himself to be more accommodating to the students.

The name on the door to room *412* read, "Professor Petula Sally." Stryker knocked once.

"Come in."

"Professor Stryker!" Petula greeted sitting at her desk. The headband was missing and her red hair glistened in the sunlight streaming through the window. She hurriedly scribbled something on a small piece of paper. "Here, clip this to the door outside, will you?" She stood and handed the note to Stryker. "And lock it when you come back in. Thank you." She sat down.

Stryker posted the note which read, "Will return in one-half hour."

Petula's office was eight by ten and was nothing elaborate. It was a bit cramped. An oak desk was covered in clear glass holding yellow chrysanthemums, writing pad, pen cup, and three textbooks. Bookshelves left of the desk held a few books, but most of the shelving space was filled with knickknacks. Lace curtains by the open window danced lazily in the breeze behind her desk.

"I have a student coming by about now. He can come back. That's why I had you lock the door. I don't want him to think I'm here." She rose, came around the desk, and extended her hand, holding on to his a little longer than necessary. "So glad we will be sharing space for a while. Would you like any coffee? I picked some up after my class. I usually do." Petula spoke rapidly, nervously. "I get a pot refilled and bring it here to my office. I have extra cups." She picked up the porcelain coffee pot and asked with elevated eyebrows, "Would you like one?"

Stryker briefly wondered if Petula was always so talkative before he answered. "Yes." The top button on her white blouse was unbuttoned, showing a hint of cleavage. *You don't need to be so obvious. Aren't there any men without bowties in this place?*

She poured coffee in a matching porcelain cup and handed it to Stryker. "Won't you please sit down?"

He accepted the dainty cup, a little awkwardly, usually having his coffee in a mug. Nevertheless, he limited his little finger action. "Petula Sally."

"Yes, I'm often asked, which is my first name and which is my last. Petula is my first name. Didn't you already know that?" She received no reply from Stryker. "Yes, of course you did. My old boyfriend called me "Pet" for short."

"Do you prefer Doctor or Professor Sally?" Stryker asked, sipping from the cup.

"Please, just call me Petula." That had a little frost on it.

Stryker noticed the temperature drop and quickly reminded himself he needed information from this woman. "All right, Petula. I like the name."

"Thank you." Warmer. "Are you from California? Edward said you attended West Point, but where were you before that?"

"I grew up in the Bay Area." He caught her looking at his left hand.

What the hell, he'd taken account of her ring finger too. So, they were both unmarried. Made it less complicated. "And yourself?" He glanced in the cup and took another sip.

"Yes, me too. I guess we have something in common. Stryker, I'm guessing that is your last name?" The inquiry brought elevated eyebrows again. "Do you have a first?"

"Neville." He tried to smile. It looked more like a snarl, but he tried.

Fortunately, Petula recognized the effort for what it was and returned the smile. "Neville, Neville Stryker. Has a good ring to it." Petula hadn't seen the weathered "Neville" on his saddle.

"Tell me about the protesters. Saw them when I came in."

"Oh, they want to change the world," Petula replied with a grin.

"Change the world."

"Make it a better place."

"I guess the world could use a little help," Stryker said with a straight face. "They're students?"

"A few. Others just want to help."

"Know any of 'em?"

"Been introduced to a few by one of my students. Seem genuine. How's the coffee?"

"Good."

"Would you like more?"

"Your student appointment."

"Yes, I forgot." Petula scrunched her face, then said, "If you're not busy, would you care to come by my apartment for dinner? We could talk more then. Get to know each other. After all, we are sharing space." The offer came with a nice smile.

"Not too much trouble?"

"No, left over stew. No trouble at all. Say around six?"

"Yes."

Petula wrote down her address, stood, and handed the note to Stryker. After he took it, she held out her hand and again held his a little longer, and a little tighter.

Stryker passed the student at the door.

Why would Petula be drawn to someone like him? He certainly

would not seem to be her type. He could not be mistaken for a disciple of good which she seems to like. And he is not what you would call handsome. His fierce countenance and ghostly pale eyes dispel any notion of that. Does Petula possibly see him as a man of strength? Stryker is not a muscular man; however, strength can be projected from character. Is she attracted to perceived power? Not the quiet, subtle power of a rich man who, with the stroke of the pen, can unleash the clout of money against another man, and ruin him financially. Not that kind of power. Stryker's power is more direct, more personnel. With the pull of a trigger or slash of a blade, he can take more than money from a man. He can take his life. All he has and all he will ever have. Does she like the kind of raw power? Or, is Petula attracted to him for another reason? One, which has a strange, or perhaps, a darker connotation? The intent of her flirtations was difficult to know. Stryker pondered these things as he walked from Petula's office.

Stryker figured he would have plenty of time to check on Tooonug and get Petula's place in Haight-Ashbury by six o'clock. The district was named after two streets, Henry Haight and Monroe Ashbury, prominent leaders of San Francisco. It had yet to gain the notoriety of the "Beat" generation. That would be seven decades later. However, after establishment of the cable car line connecting Golden Gate Park with Market Street and downtown, apartment buildings sprang up and Petula lived in one of those, commuting by ferry, as did Stryker, across the bay to Berkeley.

He hopped on a cab in front of the Ferry house. "Take me to the Embarcadero," Stryker instructed, climbing in behind the driver. "I'll tell you where to stop and wait for me when we get there." He wasn't sure about the location of Petula's apartment building. The area was new to him. It might be too far to walk and the driver would likely know the address.

They arrived at Tooonug's rooming house in the alley as darkening clouds brought an early evening. Stryker hoped Tooonug had remained in the place and hadn't wandered off, requiring time to look for him. Worse yet, gotten into trouble and would need help getting out of it. *Shit, Tooonug, you better be in this damn hole.* The Paiute was prone to fighting. He won most of them, but some of his opponents died and that was why he spent a lot of time in jail. Stryker jumped from the buggy and quickly stepped up to the front door. The door was open and he headed down the hall to Tooonug's room with building apprehension. *Shit, maybe he wasn't a good idea...* Stryker turned the doorknob, and opened the door.

Tooonug was there all right—with company. The Paiute was lying face down on the bed. A pair of female legs were wrapped around his hips, and Tooonug was humpin' and gruntin'.

Stryker stood in the doorway, dumbstruck. *Is he raping her?* He was trying to decide if he should pull Tooonug off the woman when he heard her say, "Does Tooonug like? Another half hour, five more dollars." Stryker stepped from the room and eased the door to.

"Take me to this address." Stryker handed Petula's handwritten note the cab driver. The five-mile ride took forty-five minutes to Haight-Ashbury district. Darker now, and a light rain slickened the stone pavement. Crowded streets with people going home from work made the going slow as well, that is until they almost reached Petula's apartment, where traffic thinned. Stryker paid the driver and released him. This might take a while, he thought.

Petula's apartment was on the second level. Stryker entered the building and climbed the stairs, wondering how to ask for the needed information without arousing the woman's suspicions. He walked down the hall to the last door on the right, numbered *216* in brass. No name. He rapped twice.

Stryker heard hurried footsteps inside. The door swung open. Petula had changed clothing. The headband was back. A pale green blouse replaced the white one with two top buttons now open. She wore a maroon skirt reaching past her calves. It was not as billowy as the one she'd worn in her office. It hung more tightly, it had a suggestive split which extended slightly above the knee. A multi-colored sash with streaks of red, orange, and yellow circled her narrow waist. The ends of the colorful waistband dangled down to her knees. After taking in full measure of Petula, Stryker looked around the apartment.

Lots of potted plants on tables, counters, and wall sconces. Maroon painted walls and planked wooden floors spilled from the living room into the kitchen. A plain forest green dining table with two slat-back wooden chairs constituted the dining area which separated the kitchen from the front room. Two place settings were on the table. A bamboo settee with flowered cushions, two comfortable-looking cushioned chairs, a coffee table by the settee, and a teak table between the chairs made up the rest of the furniture. Two chandeliers hung from the ceiling, one in the living room and a smaller one in the kitchen. The door to the bedroom was closed. He supposed a bathroom was somewhere else, maybe down the hall. Not bad on college pay, Stryker supposed.

"Nice apartment, Petula." Giving a compliment was a decent start.

"You like it? I decorated it myself." Petula stretched out an arm and swung in a circle. "The stew is almost ready." She pointed toward the kitchen with a friendly smile. "I just had to warm it up. Would you like a glass of wine before dinner?"

"Yes, that would be nice." *Don't be too sickening, asshole.*

Petula spun gaily about and skipped little quick steps to the kitchen cabinet. She flung it open and pulled out a bottle of red wine plus two water glasses. She filled the glasses half-way and carried them into the living room. "Here you go," she said, giving him one. "Let's sit and you can tell me about yourself." Petula plopped on the settee and patted the cushion next to her.

Stryker accepted the glass and sat on a single chair across from her.

Petula flashed a pout, then quickly erased it. "All right Neville, tell me about Mister Stryker." She smiled, crossed her legs, and sipped the wine.

"Not much to tell. Grew up in San Francisco. Attended West Point. Spent a few years in the Army and got out." Stryker drank from the glass, surprised the wine was good. "And you?"

"Me? Oh well, I grew up here too," Petula replied. "My father owned a bank and I had a good upbringing, especially since I am an only child. I may have been spoiled." She flashed an impish grin.

Stryker wondered which bank and why Petula didn't mention its name. Now he knew where she got the money for the apartment. College professor's salary probably couldn't pay for it. "You like teaching?" Lame, but he couldn't think of anything else to say.

"Love it! I get to interact with young people. Share ideas. I started a group-think get-together. At first, there were only three of us and we met here every week. That was four months ago. Now there are twenty-one, not counting myself, and we meet in a separate room at the library. We have—"

"What do you talk about?" Stryker interrupted.

"Ah well, lots of things, philosophy, politics, current events, and... oh, I think the stew must be ready by now." Petula jumped up from the settee and darted to the kitchen, setting her glass on the dining table on the way. "Take a chair at the table. I'll bring your bowl."

Stryker moved to the table, pulled out a chair, and sat. He watched Petula ladle stew into a wooden bowl. She carried it in two hands and set it in front of him. "Hope you like it." She returned to the stove, spooned out a bowl for herself and came back to the table.

He took a chance, a big one. He'd wasted too much time chasing after false leads. The fruitless out-of-town trip gnawed at him. He suspected she could provide useful information and wanted it now. He had to find out where Morgan might be, and soon.

Petula, I need your help. A girl has been kidnapped. Her life is in danger. He used "girl" to describe Morgan instead of "woman," thinking it might make Petula more helpful. "We don't know where she's being held. It's been several days now. A ransom is demanded from whoever is holding her. If not paid, they've vowed to kill her."

"Are you a policeman?" Petula was about to sip the stew, but she lowered the spoon. "I thought you might not be a real professor."

"I'm not a policeman, but I need to locate the girl." Stryker rested his elbows on the table. "Will you help?"

"How can I? I don't know anything." Petula scrunched her eyebrows. "Does Edward know about you?"

"Edward and I were at West Point together. He's agreed to help, and he thinks you might be able to as well." Stryker was climbing way out on a shaky limb.

"What do you want from me?" Petula asked, looking puzzled.

Stryker moved out to the skinny part of the limb. "We, Edward, and myself, suspect some of the protesters at school may had something to do with it. The ransom demand alludes to Marxist ideology." Stryker was leaving out police involvement on purpose. "Is there someone in the protest group you think I could talk to? Not that they are necessarily involved, but maybe they know something which might be helpful."

"I can't believe this. You're not a professor, are you?" Petula asked incredulously.

I have fucked up. "I have taught before." Stryker did not say what he taught, where, or when. "A girl's life is in real danger, Petula." He was getting aggravated, now. He might have to try a different tactic.

"I don't think anyone in our group would know anything about it." Petula got defensive.

"And I believe you," Stryker assuaged. "What about any of the protestors who might not be a student? Someone not in your group-think?"

"Your stew is getting cold."

"Petula, think," Stryker said. "Do you know who leads the protesters, for example?"

"Maybe. Maybe I do," she said coyly.

"Tell me. Who is he?" Stryker was getting impatient now. He briefly thought about flying across the table and choking the woman. "I'm desperate to save this girl's life." Stryker *was* desperate, so much so, he bordered on pleading. *Dammit woman, do I have to beg.*

"You haven't said what this girl means to you."

"We work together. I feel responsible." *Don't ask how old Morgan is.* Stryker left out Hearst's involvement. No need for heavy guns unless necessary. Thinking of the senator brought about time running short. He might be getting pressure from the kidnappers by now.

"All right, mister Stryker, if that's your real name. We will make a deal."

"Neville Stryker is real. What's your deal?"

"Don't get antsy." Petula recognized her advantage. "Let me tell you a story."

"I don't want a story, Petula."

"A fish story."

"Shit."

"Now, now. You want me to tell you a name or not?"

"Be quick."

"An old man went fishing out in a large lake. He—"

"Fish story. God-dammit, Petula—"

"Don't rush me!"

Stryker tried to settle down. Petula had the stronger hand.

"He caught his limit every time he went out to fish. No one else caught any fish at all. People wondered how he did it. What bait he used, etcetera. You fish a lot Neville?"

"Never."

"The game warden was suspicious too." Petula sipped wine from her glass prior to continuing. Probably to mess with Stryker. "So, he asked to go out with the old man one day." Petula ate a spoonful of stew. Drank more wine. "When they got out in the farthest section of the lake and away from everybody, the old man pulled out a stick of dynamite. Lit it and tossed it over the side of the boat. It exploded and dead fish rose to the surface."

"How long is this gonna—"

"Shush! And listen!" Petula sipped more wine "The warden told the old man, 'You can't do that! It's against the law!' Then the old man picked out another stick of dynamite, lit it, handed it to the game warden, and said–now get this, Neville– 'Are you gonna sit there and argue or are you gonna fish?" Petula burst out laughing at her own joke.

"Dammit, Petula!"

"Now, Mister Stryker," Petula interjected with a serious face. She paused for effect and then asked, "Are you gonna sit there and argue, or are you gonna fuck me?"

Fifteen minutes later, Stryker and Petula lay naked on her big brass bed–to consummate the deal.

Her headband discarded, Petula's auburn hair spread luxuriously on a fluffy white pillow. Her ivory body glistened on hot pink sheets. Cherry red nipples protruded a half inch atop nicely shaped, firm breasts. Farther down her lithe body, Stryker noticed she was a true redhead. *What will scratch her itch?*

"Please don't be too gentle, I've been naughty." Petula raised her arms behind her head, crossed her wrists, and laid them on the brass rail above the pillows. She offered Stryker a mischievous grin.

What's this? Daddy gifts her money and she feels guilty that the rest of the world can't eat escargot. Needs to be punished?

Stryker, lying stretched out next to Petula, grabbed her wrists in an iron grip, and pinned them against the brass.

Petula reacted with a smile and closed her eyes.

Her clothing lay nearby on the bed. Stryker's was on the floor. The long sash. He used it to tie Petula's wrists to the rail and covered her eyes with the ends. She responded with a wiggle of her hips. Settling in beside her, he slowly ran a forefinger around her breasts, flicking a nipple with each passing. The little buds grew harder. Cupping a breast, he squeezed the nipple between thumb and forefinger. The pinch prompted a high-pitched, "Ow!" He pinched the other nipple for another squeal. He pinched harder and pulled. It had to hurt. Petula moaned.

Leaving her breasts, Stryker slid his hand down the front of her body to tightly closed thighs. "Open 'em."

Petula opened her legs four inches.

"Wider."

She stretched her legs, shapely legs, wider, and Stryker took a moment to admire the two finely-toned appendages, one at a time. Long enough in fact for Petula to wonder what he was up to. Then he smacked her clitoris.

Petula took in a sharp breath and closed her legs. "That hurt."

"Open 'em."

Petula hesitated.

He kissed her lips, pinched a nipple, and whispered in her ear. "Open them."

Petula cautiously separated her thighs.

"More."

She opened wider.

Stryker felt inside. Wet. Very wet. He withdrew his fingers and smacked her clitoris again.

"Ow!" Petula writhed her wrists against the bed rail and his grip. She clasped her thighs together.

"Spread 'em!" Stryker growled.

"Ummm!" Petula's kept her mouth tightly closed, but she eased her trembling thighs open for him. *Is she frightened or aroused?*

"Want me to stop?"

"No." Petula violently shook her head back and forth. The red mane flew about the pillow. "No, don't stop."

Stryker leaned closer. Bit on a rigid nipple, but not hard enough to draw blood. He inserted three fingers, felt up an inch inside for the G-spot, momentarily caressed it, and then went deeper. Then he brought the dripping fingers to her lips again. "Lick 'em."

Petula opened her mouth. Stryker stuck his fingers between her lips, and the college professor sucked and licked.

Stryker made more trips to Petula's vagina, each time smacking her clitoris and making her lick his fingers.

By now Stryker was aroused too. He slid around and knelt between Petula's thighs. Positioning the head of his penis against her vagina, he slowly rubbed the head of it back and forth. Petula reacted by lifting her hips to take him in, but Stryker held back.

"Say please."

"Please." Petula lifted her hips again.

"Say please fuck me."

"Please fuck me." She moved up again and gave up when he wouldn't enter. "C'mon, put it in!"

"The name."

"What name?"

"The lead protester."

"Damn you, Stryker." Petula cursed, then spat, "Asher Slowick!" Now give it."

Stryker rammed hard.

"Ah, Jesus! Petula grunted and then finished with, "To me."

Stryker pumped Petula long and hard, wanting to make sure the woman got properly fucked. He spread her arms, tied her wrists to the brass rail, and took her from behind. They did it in many different positions until Petula finally said she'd had enough. He'd fulfilled his obligation while hoping he'd get more information from her, and… *all right, dammit, Petula was one hell of a good fuck.*

Stryker was no saint. You can find saints in the Bible.

Stryker doesn't consider himself good with women in bed. Never thought of himself that way. He just tries to satisfy their needs and then himself. No kitchen chairs, balloons, or heroics. Find out what the woman wants and give it to her. His job. That's what he did for Petula. If he satisfied her and got the needed information, good. Men who bedded Petula before must not have scratched her itch. Otherwise, she would not have been so eager, or… desperate. Maybe the others used kitchen chairs and balloons, and wore bowties.

"Where can I find Asher Slowick? Stryker asked. "I won't tell him about you," he added, while buttoning his shirt.

"Lives in the next apartment over there," Petula said, still lying in bed. She threw an arm in the supposed direction and then let it plop back on the sheet. Strands of red hair, drenched with sweat, were matted to her forehead. She lay resting without covering herself as Stryker dressed. The professor had had a workout.

"What's he look like?"

"You just want to talk to him?"

"I want to save the girl. If he knows where I can find her, he needs to tell me."

"Average height, thin, skinny I guess, wears horn-rimmed glasses and a pony tail most of the time."

"Age."

"Mid-twenties." Petula reached for a blanket and wrapped it around her. "Hope you find her."

Stryker left Petula's apartment thinking about Morgan. He felt guilty. He'd had his fun, yeah it was fun, and Morgan was probably suffering somewhere, or maybe even worse… maybe dead. Stryker would take out his frustrations on the Marxist bastard if, and when, he found him.

He caught a cab to the Palace. Sitting alone with his thoughts, he longed for riding the roan on a friendly trail, knowing Morgan was safe. Would that happen again? "Shit."

"You need to stop, mister?"

"No, I can wait."

Too late for dinner, he grabbed a ham biscuit and a beer from the hotel restaurant and went up to his room. No class the next day. No preparation needed tonight. He drew hot water in the tub, got in, and attempted to wash off the guilty pleasure.

The next morning, Stryker met Senator Hearst in the men's grill room for breakfast.

"Got notice from the kidnappers. They're getting impatient," Hearst warned when Stryker joined him at the table. "They gave me three days, three days to get a piece in the *Examiner,* 'to extol the virtues of socialism,' they said." He shook his head in disgust and waited for Stryker's reply. It never came. "Nothing from the commissioner. You got anything?"

"Name of a protester who might know something."

"Better talk to him soon, or else my son will have to put a piece in the paper. One more thing, Stryker. I know how you must feel about Morgan. I have… well strong inclinations myself. I've heard things about you. That you can be a little rough. I guess some of that may be of some use now, but just try to be discreet about it."

Stryker curtailed the urge to lean across the table and punch Hearst. It was the first time he'd felt that way toward the man. Stryker controlled his anger, though. He sat back to think for a minute. Maybe Hearst had his reasons. Could be he was trying to protect him from the commissioner. McGee would be watching Stryker. Probably would jump at the chance to put him in jail. McGee had no "inclinations" toward Morgan. However, Stryker knew the policeman's inclinations toward him and they weren't friendly. Stryker decided to accept that Hearst's warning was for his benefit and let it go at that. He nodded to the senator and rose from the table.

Stryker walked from the hotel and caught a cable car to the Ferry House. He was tired of riding in cabs. They reminded him of the primary reason he'd been taking them; he was in a hurry to find

Morgan. Three days wasn't much time to find out where she was being held. A sudden pang of "inclination" hit him in the chest and he realized how much she meant to him. There was only one Morgan, only one woman for him. She could not be replaced. Before Morgan, he'd never given much thought to politics or philosophy. Morgan changed that. She taught him about the virtue of truth and reason, and concepts juxtaposed to what he had been told as a youth, like "Share with others; don't be selfish." In Egalitaria, the town leaders promoted the slogan, "From each according to his ability, to each according to his need." Morgan said giving should be voluntary, not required by anybody. That no one has the right to take from a person and give to another. She said political leaders do it, but by what right? "Who gave them that right?" She asked him. Marxist thugs took over the town, killed her husband, and confiscated her ranch and mine. She experienced their thuggery first-hand and despised it. Stryker realized early on how special Morgan was, not just for their lovemaking, but for her ideals. She made him feel different about things. This newly discovered philosophy Morgan gave him seemed... so right. It was as if he suddenly awoke to a fresh clean way to live. Stryker had never bowed to any man and Morgan's words easily struck home. She needed to live. *Her ideals must survive.* A shudder went through him. He'd do anything to find her. McGee can go to hell.

At the Ferry House, Stryker retrieved the roan. He and the horse took the ferry ride to Alameda. He was not sure why he chose to bring the roan. Could be if he should need to leave the Bay Area, he might need the horse. The five "Ps," prior planning prevents piss-poor performance. If counting the words, piss-poor is hyphenated. Or, he didn't want to get in another cab. Stryker rode the horse to the college.

Protestors were out in force when he arrived on campus. Asher wasn't difficult to find. He was out in front holding a sign that read, "Power to the People" and repeated slogans along with others such as "Unite Against Tyranny" and more tripe Marxists revolutionaries use. *It is surprising, puzzling, how many seemingly bright people are taken in by that shit,* Stryker thought. *Dim wits, useful idiots, don't know any better, but intelligent people? Why Socialism?* He had witnessed first-hand in Egalitaria[i] how utopian egalitarianism worked under that system. It worked at the point of a gun.

He wondered how he would isolate Asher for interrogation. Stryker had a plan for the questioning, but not for getting Asher alone. Also, for the nasty persuasion, Stryker might need Tooonug. Stryker was known for many things, bad things, evil things, but he was no torturer. It was not in him. A quick, efficient kill, that's how he dealt with assholes. For Morgan? Well, maybe he *could* torture a man. He would take no pleasure in it. He gave himself twelve hours to get Asher with Tooonug before he, Stryker, made a more desperate move.

At the apartment. After recognizing Slowick from Petula's description, Stryker figured the apartment might afford the best opportunity to get him alone. He wheeled the roan about and rode on up to North Hall. After hitching the roan, he entered the building and took the stairs to Petula's office. It was a long shot. Have Petula garner a meeting with Asher. Act nice and ask for his help to locate Morgan. A real long shot. He was willing to do anything, including acting nice. *It also included killing the fucker.*

She wasn't in. *Odd*, he thought. She had a class that morning and she usually spent time making final preparations for it in her office. He checked the classroom. It was empty. Stryker wasn't sure why he wanted to see her. Being on campus though, maybe in the back of his mind he thought she might at least give him more information. Worth a try. He asked a couple of staff members if they had seen her. No one had.

Stryker rode the roan back to Alameda to catch a return ferry to San Francisco. He had an uneasy twitch in the gut. Sure, attempting to arrange a friendly meeting with the three of them, Stryker, Asher, and Petula seemed improbable, but you never know. Stranger things have happened, but not this time.

President Holden met Stryker at the ferry dock in Alameda. He had just handed over the roan to load when Holden approached him. The college president wore a grim look.

"A word with you, Stryker," Holden whispered, taking Stryker by the elbow, and guiding them away from the crowd. "Bad news. They found Professor Sally's body in front of her apartment early this morning."

"Shit!"

"That's what I said when I heard," Holden said. She'd been beaten up something awful. Whoever did it must have had it in for her. She made it out to the yard before she died. The apartment was a wreck and it looks like the beating happened in there."

"Was the front door damaged?" Stryker asked.

"No, it wasn't. The police sergeant thinks she may have let in whoever killed her. Appears she may have known them. That's according to the sergeant, anyway."

"Any idea who did it?" Stryker's face darkened.

"Nothing was taken, so burglary doesn't seem to be the motive. If it were, they probably wouldn't take the time to beat her up like they did."

"They."

"Evidence suggests more than one killer. Bruises on both wrists point to her being held while she was beaten." Holden was taking deep breaths now. He looked drained, worried, fearful. Petulla's killing appeared to hang heavy on him. "Marks on her wrists don't match with being tied. Police are sure more than one person did it."

"Maybe it's related," Stryker growled.

"What's related?" Holden asked. Eyebrows scrunched; head cocked. "Petula and Morgan?"

"And more." Stryker immediately regretted saying too much, and walked away, leaving Holden standing with a question on his face.

Stryker melted into the crowd and boarded the ferry. He stood by an outside rail to think. Were things falling into place? He suspected Petula's murder and Morgan's kidnapping *were* connected, and Asher Slowick had some talking to do. *Who's behind this all this shit?* The kidnapping, murder, and the protests. Someone must be organizing the protests, maybe paying protesters. They could be paying for Slowick's apartment too. Petula didn't mention he worked anywhere. These suspicions swirled around in Stryker's head. He shoved them aside and struck a plan.

When the ferry reached San Francisco, Stryker pulled the lariat off the roan and had the horse stabled at the Ferry House. Bringing it wasn't needed after all. Stryker's expression hardened. No more time for mistakes.

Next to the turntable were eight oxbow wagons with hitched horses, lined up and ready for rent. Stryker sought out the owner and finally found him inside the Ferry house having coffee in the deli.

"Five dollars for the night. Bring it back here at six in the morning. Late fee is fifty cents an hour. I need a deposit," the crusty old man grunted. He took another gulp of coffee. "What you gonna use it for?"

"Hauling trash."

"Bring it back clean. It's another two dollars if I have to clean it."

"What's the deposit?" Stryker asked, his irritation rising to a dangerous level.

"Twenty-five dollars. You'll get it back if everything is in order."

"No. My horse is in the stables there." Stryker thumbed over his shoulder at the ferry stables. The stable boy can point him out. If I don't bring your wagon back, you can keep him. "He's my deposit. Worth more than a wagon and nag you got out front." Stryker now looked menacing enough to encourage an agreement.

"I reckon that'll be all right. Take whichever one you want."

Stryker went outside, climbed on a wagon, and snapped the reins to start down Market Street.

The sun plopped into the Pacific by the time Stryker hopped from the wagon at Tooonug's rooming house. He missed seeing the fiery splash.

Luckily, Tooonug had no company when Stryker burst through the door. "Let's go."

The Paiute leaped out of bed and put on the top hat. "Tooonug ready."

"Take off the suit. Put on the buckskins."

Tooonug tore off the suit, and quickly put on the buckskin breech-cloth, leggings, and beaded shirt. He stuffed the knife in his belt. "Tooonug ready." Sitting in the tiny room and waiting was boring for an Indian used to being outdoors. His wait was only interrupted once because he didn't have enough money for more interruptions. Boredom didn't sit well with the Paiute. He was eager to get out of the small room.

Outside, Stryker and Tooonug climbed onto the driver's bench and they headed for Haight-Asbury. The Paiute sat silently beside Stryker. It was difficult to guess what was going through the Indian's mind. He had seen much and suffered much. He had endured more than his share of tragedy. Still, he seemed reconciled to his life. His one friend, if Stryker qualified as one, sat beside him. The two men communicated more by not speaking, each more comfortable in silence rather than making idle conversation.

Stryker reined the nag to a stop at the corner of Haight and Ashbury, and the two men stepped from the wagon. Stryker took a moment to recall how Petula lay positioned in bed after sex, and in what direction she pointed when he asked where Asher lived. He started toward the building left of Petula's apartment. Tooonug followed.

Two policemen stood near a taped-off area in front of Petula's apartment. Stryker did not stop to talk. He suspected he knew more about her death than they did. The policemen rolled up the tape, got in the police wagon, and drove away. The apartment house stood two hundred feet north of Petula's. There was no moon, and no lights lit the dirt path for Stryker and Tooonug to the three-story apartment building. They climbed three steps to the front door and entered.

Stryker found a wood placard in the foyer with a list of names and numbers next to the names. The address board was half full with only two names listed on the second floor. Slowick was one, number *206*. *First and third floors being the most desirable*, Stryker guessed. The ground floor for convenience and the third for the view. They climbed the stairs to the second floor. Kerosene lanterns burned in the hallway, providing light to read the numbers. Room *206* was down the hall on the left.

Stryker knocked on the door. There was no answer. He knocked again and got nothing. He tried the copper doorknob. It turned and he opened the door to the one-room apartment. Wood floors were sparsely furnished with a kitchen table and two chairs, two single beds by the side walls, and two straight-back chairs near each bed. That was it. There were no cabinets by the table. No storage of any kind. Only bare walls, and the only lighting was a lantern on the table. Another lantern on a chair wasn't lit. Poster boards with the familiar Marxist slogans painted on them were strewn about on the table and the floor. What was missing? Stryker realized it was clothes. *Why were there no clothes?* Must be a meeting room for planning protests. Anger raged inside the mixed breed– *Don't kill the Slovick until he talks, dammit. When will the fucker return?* Stryker had a few questions.

Stryker grabbed a chair and placed it by the door. He motioned for Tooonug to do the same. Tooonug lifted the chair and something rolled off to clang on the floor. Tooonug ignored it, but Stryker bent down and picked up the eighteen-inch iron pipe. He took it to the lantern light. It was caked blood on one end. He carried the pipe and sat on a chair by the door. Tooonug sat across from him.

After a half hour, they heard someone come down the hall, pausing every few steps. *Checking the lamps*, Stryker figured. Three more hours passed. During that entire time, neither man spoke. They sat and waited. Finally, there were footfalls in the hall accompanied by two males talking.

The noise stopped outside the door. "Gotta get up early, Hernan." The door opened.

Asher caught the pipe in the mouth, knocking two teeth down his throat. Stryker kneed Asher in the gut, doubling him over. The pipe hit struck again, just beneath the back of Slovick's skull. Stunned, Asher fell to the floor. Tooonug had his knife on the second man's throat, waiting for Stryker to say, "Kill him."

Slowick lay on the floor moaning. Stryker stepped to the second man and smashed his nose with the pipe.

Tooonug held Hernan up, holding the knife to his throat. "You hit again."

Stryker obliged.

The boy's legs buckled. He spread his feet to remain standing.

Stryker swung the pipe, bringing it up into Hernan's groin. "Let him fall."

Tooonug pulled the knife away and Hernan dropped to his knees, blood pouring from his nose.

"Here, cut four pieces of rope, Stryker said, handing the lariat to Tooonug. "Tie their arms. Make it tight. Then sit them up."

Tooonug was an expert at roping enemy captives; he made the bindings snug. They would not wiggle free.

Tooonug bent over each moaning man, tugged at the ropes, and straightened. "Rope tight. They not get loose."

Stryker stripped wool blankets from both beds and draped one over each man. The two men sat cross-legged and accepted the coverings without moving. Not able to see the pipe, neither man invited another blow. Stryker picked up a cut piece of rope and tied it around Asher at his waist level. Tooonug did the same with Hernan.

"Stay here with them. I'll be back soon. I'll knock three times."

Stryker opened the door. He checked the hallway and then walked to the stairs. So far, the commotion in *206* hadn't raised any suspicions. He saw no one downstairs either. He opened the front door. *Shit!* He had hoped not to run into anybody when they brought out Slovick and Hernan. Two young men, one skinny and one fat, stood by the wagon. They talked in hushed tones, but loud enough for Stryker to hear their discussion.

"Let's take it to carry signs and shit."

"Who's is it? Never seen it here before."

"Who give's a shit. They left it out here to get stolen. Besides, if we bring it back, it ain't stealin'. It's borrowing."

"Maybe Asher got it for us."

"Hey, you ain't as dumb as you look. C'mon, let's ask him."

"Don't think he's back yet."

"Said he'd leave the door unlocked and to wait for him if we beat him back."

"Evening," Stryker said, walking up to the two boys. The skinny one was also short; the fat one was a bit taller. Both wore long hair past their shoulders.

"Uhhh, sir!" Startled, the boys hadn't heard Stryker's approach. After stuttering the greeting, the boy asked, "This your horse and wagon?"

"Belongs to the fellow in room *206*, I think." Stryker pulled the sai. Keeping it behind his back, he stepped closer.

"Oh, do you know if he's home?"

Stryker swung the sai. The center tine struck the skinny kid's temple.

A quarter turn of the sai and a wing tine punctured his left eye. He staggered a few steps and fell under the wagon. Stryker attacked the fat one. He turned to run and Stryker caught him from behind. He got a hand under the boy's chin and lifted it. Then he swung the sai in front and drove the center tine through the kid's tracheal notch. The tine broke skin behind the boy's neck, and he collapsed to the ground, gagging and spewing blood out the hole in his throat.

Stryker turned back to the skinny youth to finish him. No need. The commotion startled the horse. It pulled the wagon forward and a wheel rolled over his neck. By the time Stryker loaded him in the wagon, the fat one finished dying, and he muscled him in too. Stryker climbed in the wagon and rode several blocks until he came to a dark deserted alley. There, he dumped the bodies and turned the wagon around.

Stryker once knew a man who owned a large malamute sled dog. The man told the story of when the dog was half-grown, it curiously approached a cat. The feline clawed the dog's eye. The malamute killed it. Broke the cat's back with one bite. After that, the dog killed every cat it found. Stryker did the same with Marxists.

CHAPTER TEN

Stryker encountered no more protesters when he returned to the apartment. He rapped his knuckles three times on the door and Tooonug cracked it open. Upon seeing Stryker, he swung it wider.

Stryker saw Asher and Hernan sitting quietly under the blankets and growled, "On your feet, boys. You're going for a ride."

Stryker grabbed the pipe, then he and Tooonug helped the two men to their feet. Stryker, grabbed the blanket at the back of Asher's neck, dragged him to the door, and opened it. He searched up and down the hall, and seeing no one, he pulled Asher out behind him. Tooonug brought out Hernan. Stryker waited until all four were in the hall and quietly eased the door to. He led Asher to the stairs and guided him down the steps. Tooonug and Hernan followed. Asher recovered a bit of courage going down the stairs and he mouthed words around the gag, attempting to ask where they were going. He stopped trying when Stryker hit him with the pipe.

Notorious Bay Area fog made its appearance, creeping up the streets like a monstrous creature crawling from the sea. Stryker led Asher around back of the wagon and bent his upper body forward and onto the bed. "Grab a leg, Tooonug." With Stryker on one leg Tooonug the other, they shoved Asher into the wagon. Then they loaded Hernan.

"Ride with them in the back. Make sure the boys don't fall out." Stryker knew the sarcasm was lost on Tooonug. The instructions were for the two men's benefit. They shouldn't get any ideas about trying to escape. Tooonug saw the blood in the wagon and said nothing.

Long years had passed since Stryker roamed the streets of San Francisco in his youth; however, he calculated taking Castro Street south he would run into 25th Street and then take it east to the isolated cove. Street signs were either missing or difficult to read in the fog. Stryker kept the horse at a modest pace. The three men behind him in the wagon maintained their silence, allowing Stryker to mull over what to do with the young Marxists. He had already planned a bad ending, if or, when they told him what he wanted to know. Now that he knew them to be Petula's killers, he figured they needed a proper send-off. Tooonug could help with that. The four-mile trip took about forty-five minutes. They found the boat where he'd left it. Out in the bay, ships blew fog horns, eerie warnings to stay clear of one another. Stryker dragged the boat to the water while Tooonug stood between Asher and Hernan, holding them by gripping their blankets. By now, knowing they were near water and having heard the boat scrapping across the sand, they might have thought they were being shanghaied.

"Get 'em in the boat," Stryker ordered.

Tooonug shoved Asher and Hernan forward. Stryker held the boat steady in knee-deep water while Tooonug helped each man into the boat. Small waves lapped against the bow, rocking it, and Stryker braced his hip against the gunwale. "Put them here," he said, patting the stern thwart with his hand.

Tooonug got both men seated on the end bench seat and sat on the center thwart, facing them.

Stryker stepped into the boat. "Set them in front, Tooonug." The Paiute maneuvered around Stryker to the front thwart. Tooonug had not ridden in a row boat before; however, he had spent many hours in canoes and knew how to keep a boat steady while moving about. Stryker took the middle, picked up the oars, placed them in the oar crutches, and started rowing.

There was little wind in the bay and the water was calm. Stryker rowed out roughly three-hundred yards and stopped. The thick fog made it impossible to see anything, much less the shoreline, but he kept the ship horns behind him. Stryker pulled the pipe from his belt "Tooonug, make them kneel here," thumping the pipe on a boat plank. "Take off their blankets and gags."

Tooonug held on to Stryker's shoulder and climbed around him. He pulled each man from the bench seat and onto his knees, facing Stryker. Using his knife, Tooonug cut off the ropes and lifted the blankets. He untied the gags but left their hands tied behind them.

"What are you gonna do with us?" Asher asked in a shaky voice. He was plenty scared. Hernan remained silent, letting Asher talk–and get hit with the pipe.

"Where's the kidnapped woman?"

"I didn't want to do it!" Hernan's nose resembled a bloody mushroom. He sniffed blood which still ran from his nose and yelled, "He made me!" Hernan nodded toward Asher.

"Shut up, Hernan!" Asher retorted. But he kept his voice down, trying not to invite the pipe.

"Where is she?" Stryker held the pipe as if he couldn't wait to swing it.

"She's in her apartment. That's the last we saw her." Asher slobbered through his missing teeth. He must have counted on Stryker not knowing Petula was dead.

Wrong woman, Asher. "Not Petula. You killed her."

Asher and Hernan remained silent.

"Who's behind the protests?"

"We don't know nothing." Asher was quick with a reply. Too quick, maybe.

"Who's paying you?" Stryker trained his eyes on Hernan.

"Asher. He gives us money."

"Hernan! Shut the fuck up!" Asher's bloody spit hit Stryker's boots.

"Tooonug, Hernan needs a haircut," Stryker said in a flat monotone. Tooonug was no barber, but he knew how to give haircuts. Close ones. Stryker now figured Hernan didn't know anything. Maybe he could still be useful though… with how he died.

Tooonug grasped Stryker's intentions. He grabbed Hernan around the neck from behind and pulled him back against his chest. Taking the knife, Tooonug scored a line around Hernan's head. Starting just above the left ear, he drew the blade to the front and across Hernan's forehead below the hairline, onto the right side, passing over the right ear, and completing the circle all the way the head to the left ear again.

"Ow! That hurts! Hernan yelled.

Tooonug fisted a handful of hair, pulled on it, and began scalping Hernan. He sawed the knife front to back, scalping swiftly. The blade was sharp and Hernan screamed as Tooonug cut. The desperate shriek carried across the bay. Three hundred yards away on shore, a covey of birds took flight. When it was done, Tooonug held up his prize and asked Stryker, "You want?"

"No. Throw it and him over."

Tooonug tossed the scalp in the water. He cupped his hands under the armpits of the still screeching man and lifted. Once Hernan was nearly upright, he shoved him over the side. Hernan kicked his legs, treading water for several minutes before he disappeared in the fog. Off in the distance, they heard him choke on the salt water. Then nothing.

"Now Slowick, tell me his name," Stryker growled, slapping the pipe in his palm.

"Gunther Sordid," Asher said. He wiped his mouth on his shoulder. "Don't scalp me! I'm telling you true!"

"Prove it."

"Never met him. He just puts money for me in the bank, Bank of California, on California Street." Asher again spit over the side of the boat this time. "They tell me how much I can take out. I have to show how I spend…" Asher coughed and spit. He'd started bleeding more.

"Where can I find him?"

"Don't know."

Stryker suspected Slowick wasn't telling all. "Not good enough. You're going to die out here. How you die is up to you."

Asher straightened, stared at Stryker with wide eyes. "All I know is he lives in a castle north of San Francisco. The bank man, Clarence, told me. Said he's rich."

"A castle," Stryker repeated. "Why the Marxist shit?"

"Told you, I ain't never met him." Asher shook uncontrollably now. "Please, I don't know no more!"

"Scalp him."

"Wait! Stop! Money! Pays money! Oh God! Help me!" Asher shrieked and tried to leap from the boat.

Stryker hit him with the pipe, knocking him unconscious. "Kill him."

Tooonug lifted Asher's chin and ran the knife across his throat and Slowick was heaved into a saltwater grave.

Stryker re-oriented the boat, putting the ship's fog horns off the stern, and rowed back to shore. Upon making land, Stryker and Tooonug dragged the boat onto the beach, far enough away from the tides, but they left it in the open. They climbed in the wagon, sitting side by side now, and rode to the Ferry House. During the ride, Stryker asked out loud, "How hard will it be to find a castle?"

Tooonug said nothing. He didn't know anything about castles.

After returning the wagon and learning when the next ferry left for Vallejo, they took a horse cab to the Palace Hotel.

"Wake him!" Stryker ordered the desk clerk. He pulled the Peacemaker to bolster the request. At first, the attaché had balked at disturbing Senator Hearst. However, he complied this time. Finally, after three tries, Hearst came on the speaking tube and the desk clerk told him about Stryker, and the gun. The gun provided the attaché an excuse to the senator for waking him at three-thirty in the morning.

"Please go right up, sir." After giving Stryker permission to see Hearst, the attaché went on a break.

Stryker left Tooonug in his room and continued down the hall to the senator's suite. The Paiute would be an unnecessary distraction.

. . .

"A castle?" Hearst asked. He'd met Stryker at the door wearing a forest-green, silk robe over same-colored pajamas. "A castle," Hearst repeated. "I'd heard some nut built one. Come in, Stryker."

"Where?"

"Somewhere in wine country. Napa Valley, I think." Hearst ran a hand through his thinning hair and pulled out a chair by the conference table. "Sit, and tell me why you think Morgan's being held in a castle."

Stryker yanked out a chair and threw himself in it. You know about Petula?"

"Yes, I heard. Tragedy."

"Protesters at the college killed her." Stryker scooted closer to the table and laid his forearms on the finely polished mahogany. "I'd been up-front with her about the kidnapping and she agreed to help. She gave me the name of the protest leader. Said he might know something."

"That was good of her."

"Yes, and I think that's why they killed her."

"The castle. She tell you about that too?"

"No, the protester did."

"That was nice of him to help. Kinda surprises me, though. I wouldn't have suspected—"

"Do you know of a man named, Gunther Sordid?" Stryker interrupted.

"Never heard of the man, why?"

"Need to talk with him. He's been providing monies to fund the protests. Find out what you can at the Bank of California. There's a teller named Clarence who may know him."

"Where are you gonna be?" Hearst asked.

"Gonna find the castle." Stryker pushed away from the table and stood. "Also, send a man to the cove at the end of 25th Street to get a boat. Have him take it back to the Embarcadero. Boat rental at the north end."

"You leaving this morning?"

"Six o'clock ferry. Send a telegram to the Vallejo telegraph office. Let me know what you find out about Sordid." Stryker walked from the room, leaving the senator sitting at the table.

Another person might wonder how Stryker got away with ordering Hearst around. First, Hearst realized Stryker was a desperate man with little time to save Morgan. Second, Hearst was fond of Morgan as well, willing to forebear Stryker's eccentricities to save her life. And lastly, he knew neither money nor political power could protect a man alone in a room from an angry Stryker.

Stryker managed two-and-a-half fitful hour's rest in the hotel room. He slept in the bed. Tooonug stretched out on the carpet. At fifteen minutes after five, Stryker rose and donned his denim, leaving the suit on the chair where he had thrown it. He and Tooonug left the room and took the elevator down to the lobby. Stryker grabbed a cup of coffee from a table that had been set out with porcelain urn cups for early-rising guests. Tooonug tried black tea. They blew on the brews to cool them enough to drink quickly and went to the roundabout to hail a horse cab. It was more crowded than Stryker expected and a long line of people waited for the cabs.

"C'mon, Tooonug," Stryker growled. "Let's go outside." He led outside, walked up to a cab driver, and waved a five-dollar bill. They arrived at the Ferry House ten minutes later.

Another queue awaited them at the Vallejo ticket window. Not a long one though. The ticket line to Alameda was much longer. More travelers headed east than north. Even more traveled on the Central Pacific to San Jose and south to Los Angeles. The Ferry House bustled with travelers, even before six o'clock and sunrise. The ferry ride to Vallejo was slightly over thirty miles and it took two and a half hours. It was agonizingly slow for a man in a rush. Thick fog lingered over the bay resulting in ferry boats that would have to temper speeds, adding to Stryker's frustration. He bought tickets for himself, Tooonug, and the roan. They would take a train heading north out of Vallejo, and somewhere along the way, rent a horse for the Paiute.

At a quarter to six, they boarded the ferry, a midship paddlewheel steamship, a double-decker boat, enclosed on the first deck, and open-air on the top level. The roan had already been led on the boat by a ferry hand, down the stern ramp to the lower level, and placed in a stall. A cold drizzle hurried passengers inside the first deck. Stryker and Tooonug found open bench space by a window. Center benches in horizontal rows, perpendicular to wall benches, ran stern to bow, interrupted by a food and drink galley mid-ship. The ferry was roughly two-thirds full with travelers scattered mostly among the center benches where boat rocking was less noticeable. The passengers consisted of single men, most of them in suits, couples young and old, and a few families with children. Stryker, not that he cared, saw no females traveling alone.

Rain poured outside the glass windows, obstructing views of the bay. The ferry eased away from the dock and was underway before Stryker realized they were moving. Once out in the bay, the ferry boat rocked gently side to side, adding weight to sleep-deprived eyelids. Stryker and Tooonug did a little nodding too.

They had been out about an hour, when a little girl, maybe six or seven years old approached Tooonug, and she put out her hand and shook his knee. "Are you a real Indian?" she asked with a cocked head and furrowed brow. The thin wisp of a girl had short cropped hair, an unbuttoned wool coat, and a faded blue dress underneath.

Tooonug who had been softly snoring with a dropped chin, top hat tilted perilously forward, pushed back the hat, and stared at the girl. He didn't answer.

"Well, are you?" she insisted.

Tooonug stared blankly, not knowing how to answer if he were real.

"Is he your Indian?" The precocious girl directed her attention to Stryker.

"No. He's Paiute. Friendly most time, and scalps heads on occasion." Stryker supplied a straight-faced answer. "Best leave him alone."

"Why does he wear that hat?"

Tooonug continued looking at her.

"Where's your parents?" Stryker wanted them to come take her away.

"My mother is dead. My father is at the bar." She pointed at the small crowd standing by the bar.

"Go away."

"My name is Florence Nightingale Graham," Florence announced with considerable pride. When she saw Stryker and Tooonug weren't impressed, she added, "Someday I'm gonna be rich." And she triumphantly walked back to sit near the bar, presumably to keep an eye on her father.

Tooonug grunted and lowered the top hat. Stryker picked up a discarded *San Francisco Examiner* to read.

Florence was true to her word. In adulthood, she changed her name for business purposes and started a highly successful cosmetics company with salons in North and South America, across Europe, and in Australia. Born December 31, 1881, and she died October 18, 1966. She owned and raced thoroughbred racehorses, and at one time had the top money-winning stable in the country. One of her horses, Jet Pilot, won the 1947 Kentucky Derby. Her net worth at death was $1.3 billion. She was the richest woman in the United States when she died. Her business name was Elizabeth Arden.

The ferry ride to Vallejo dragged on for Stryker. He felt as if he could hear Morgan calling, and sensed he was on the right path at last. He got to his feet and walked out on the deck. Tooonug followed. The fog kept him from seeing much beyond the bow, though. The ferry blew its fog horn constantly and a second boat answered in the mist ahead. Unseen it came on and eventually passed close by. He heard waves slosh against the other ferry's bow, its fog horn blasting loud and close. Then, the boat passed and horn warnings faded away in the mist.

"You bad troubled?" Tooonug stood next to Stryker peering into the fog.

Stryker turned to the Paiute. "We're running out of time to find the woman."

"We find her," Tooonug said to the fog. "Tooonug kill man who have her."

Stryker seldom if ever felt beholden to another man, but now he did. The man beside him had found his own woman impaled on a sharp tree branch to kill herself. She had been unspeakably tortured for days by Utes. Males, and especially cruel females, meted out punishment for her being an attractive Paiute woman who rejected tribal males. She was violently raped anyway and then turned over to the females. Yes, Tooonug had known tragedy. Yes, he was a violent man. He and Stryker had things in common.

The two men remained on the deck not speaking again until much later when the ferry began to slow. A faint outline of the dock and a building appeared through the mist, a sign they were arriving in Vallejo, and maybe finally, the heavy fog was lifting.

The ferry swung around and docked. Stryker and Tooonug were the first to disembark. Stryker took the roan's halter strap when it came off the boat and they headed to the train station.

"We want tickets to the castle," Stryker said to the ticket clerk standing behind brass window bars, economizing his words as usual.

"Castle." The clerk, a fiftyish, short balding fellow with a well-trimmed mustache, repeated. "No town called Castle that I know of." He took notice of Stryker's menacing countenance and quickly added with a facial twitch, "You mean a real castle?"

Stryker's hand wandered down to the Colt.

The clerk saw it and offered, "I did hear some fellow built one up near Calistoga. About forty miles north of here. Napa Valley Railroad runs up there. Central Pacific owns it now, though." He acted way more compliant now.

"What's the man's name?"

"Don't know, sir."

"Ever hear the name Gunther Sordid?"

The clerk shook his head. "No."

"Two tickets and one for the horse to Calistoga. When's the train leaving?"

"Two tickets. One horse." The clerk tore tickets from two different rolls, stamped them, and slipped them under the window bars to Stryker. "Leaves at a quarter past eleven." He glanced at the wall clock on his right. "You have two hours."

"Need a horse to rent or buy."

"There's a stable at the edge of town behind the station. Good day, sir." The nervous clerk stepped away from the window.

Stryker took the roan's strap from the rail and led it around the station. Tooonug followed. They found the stable where the station clerk had told them and were able to rent a bay gelding that was about eight years old. The fee was three dollars a day, four days in advance, and a twenty-dollar deposit that was returned when the horse was brought back. No need for a saddle. A saddle blanket, bit, and bridle were all the Paiute needed. They came back to the train station, bought another horse ticket, and still had over an hour's wait for the Napa Valley train.

Before long, more passengers gathered in the station for the ride to Napa Valley, including couples, families, and a few singles, men, and women. Stryker knew there had been mining in the area; however, none of the travelers looked like miners. Sitting with Tooonug, he picked up on their conversations which spoke of wines and hot springs. Tourists, going to Napa Valley for wine and hot baths. He even heard about a balloon ride. Stryker suddenly felt times were changing, leaving his kind behind. He was on the train, but he didn't belong on it. He heard nothing about a castle, though. He did learn the hot springs mentioned were near Calistoga. *Something to do with a castle?*

Listening in on conversations did seem to make the time pass quicker, and Stryker was a little surprised when the Central Pacific rolled into the station on time. He and Tooonug watched the horses get loaded in the cattle car, and then they climbed aboard one of the three coach cars. Stryker saw his preferred seat in the rear was empty and they made their way down the aisle. The bench across from them was not taken. An hour later the train rolled into Napa with a population of roughly four thousand. They stopped for a fifteen-minute break. Six passengers rose to leave. Looking out the window, Stryker saw several more passengers waiting on the platform to board. Tourists. If he were able to find Morgan and rescue her, what would the future hold for them in this changing world? He still pondered these ruminations after the train lurched forward, leaving the Napa station.

In a half hour, they stopped in Yountville. It was a smaller town than Napa, but it had the same grape crowd. Stryker felt more desolated. He and Tooonug weren't wine drinkers or hot tub enthusiasts, and neither had ridden a hot air balloon.

Stryker and Tooonug remained on the train. The next stop was St

Helena with a population of eighteen hundred, and it was the last town before Calistoga. It consisted of more grape fields and more wineries. Stryker thought about stepping off there and getting a cup of coffee, then figured it to be a waste of time. Probably have wine in the coffee pots. Maybe when he finds this Sordid fellow, they can sit together in a Calistoga spa, sip wine, and talk things out. No, that won't happen. Instead, Stryker thought about how he was going to kill him.

Calistoga, hot springs spa and winery, population four-hundred and twenty-three. Stryker hoped Gunther Sordid is one of them. He and Tooonug got off the train and collected the horses. After securing them to a hitching rail, they went looking for somebody who knew about a castle. The first person they asked was the ticket clerk at the train station. "Yes, there is a castle. Very secretive. It's a half-day ride east toward Lake Berryessa. Better be careful. Strangers are not welcome. Heard they shoot people," the helpful clerk told them with a warning.

Not taking time for food and drink, Stryker and Tooonug rode out of Calistoga heading east. The two men rode side by side, each keeping his own counsel. Had the ride been for recreation instead of Morgan's attempted rescue, the countryside over which they rode would probably been more enjoyable, taking in beautiful scenery of rolling hills, lush meadows, varied plant life, colorful flowers, bushes, and trees. The views were wasted on Stryker and Tooonug.

A mid-afternoon mild breeze stirred as they approached the seventeen-foot elevation of Howell Mountain and the tiny settlement of Angwin. Edwin Angwin bought several hundred acres in 1875 to build a resort. Stryker figured the climb up to the community would be worth it if someone had information about the castle. He and Tooonug stopped in front of the largest house, a two-story white-painted clapboard home.

The front screen door swung open and a bearded, hatless man who appeared in his late fifties and with sharp angular facial features stepped out on the gray-painted planked porch. "What you want here?"

"A castle," Stryker replied. He and Tooonug stayed mounted.

"Hmmm, you know those people, do you?" The man on the porch stroked his beard.

"No. I'm looking for someone that could be in the castle."

"They ain't too friendly. You could get shot at." The fellow stopped stroking his chin and wagged forefinger. "Supposed to be in the wine business, but I don't see how. No vineyard."

"Where's the castle?"

"That way," the man supplied, wagging the finger southeast. "Las Posadas Forest in the Mayacamas Mountains. Maybe a couple of miles or a little more. Ain't far. Good luck." He turned, opened the screen door, and went back into the house.

"We'll find the castle and get inside after dark," Stryker swung the roan around and headed down the hill on Howell Mountain Road in a southeasterly direction. Tooonug caught up and rode beside him.

"Look for a trail or road somewhere between here and that mountain." Stryker traced an arc across the horizon with his arm. "Should be a road between St. Helena and the castle." Stryker let the roan work its way down the hill from Angwin. Four hours of daylight left, which was time enough to find the castle, provided they could find the road to it.

The road turned right as they rode past a waterfall, and Stryker guided them left over rolling hills with thick growths of oak and manzanita trees. They came upon a well-used road that Stryker calculated ran from St Helena to the Posadas Forest up on the mountain, and they took it. The road bypassed a small lake and then it steepened, winding through taller trees, and gaining altitude.

Stryker scanned the road ahead, looking for other travelers. He glanced at Tooonug and saw him being watchful as well.

Farther up, the road spilled into an open meadow, and there Stryker saw the castle. A stone keep castle, looming large, larger than he expected. Then again, he hadn't thought much about the size and features of the castle, or how to get inside. He only wanted to find it. *Now there it is, and how do we get in the damn thing?* Stryker and Tooonug had no experience storming castles.

"We leave the horses here." Stryker dismounted and led the roan to a manzanita tree. He swapped out the bridle for a halter and looped it around a branch. Tooonug secured the bay near the roan. "We go through the woods to the castle," Stryker said, lowering his voice. "Find some way in without being seen. Here, take the carbine. You lead." Stryker pulled the Winchester from the scabbard and handed it to Tooonug. He noticed Tooonug replaced the top hat with a deer hide band to hold back his hair.

Tooonug took the carbine and weaved his way through the under-brush of berry bushes, low-level manzanita, and prickly thorn bushes. Stryker marveled at how the Paiute swam through the ground cover, hardly stirring a leaf and moving stealthily. Occasionally, Stryker snapped a twig with his boot, or brushed too closely against a bush, making a swishing sound. Tooonug ignored the paleface's lack of stealthiness.

Tooonug stopped. Stryker, looked down where he stepped, trying not to make noise, and almost ran into him. "We look," Tooonug whispered. He knelt and crawled forward to lie under two berry bushes. Stryker crawled next to him.

The huge castle squatted on a hilltop motte, a natural grass knoll where no trees had to be felled. Peering through the foliage, Stryker esti-mated the stone structure to be a rectangular five hundred by six hundred feet. He and Tooonug remained hidden roughly forty feet away from the clearing with a view of the right front corner of the castle. Monstrous, dark, sinister… and imposing. *Morgan's in that place.* Stryker tightened his jaw. Forty-foot-tall circular towers at the corners, and a smaller bastion tower stood in the middle of the right outside wall. He suspected a matching tower on the left wall. The front had two massive iron reinforced doors instead of a drawbridge Stryker had read about with medieval castles. There was no moat on top of a hill. The doors were closed, but the road which ran up to the doors appeared well-used.

"Not getting in unless they open those doors for someone coming in or out," Stryker whispered. "Let's move around back. Should be another door or gate."

He and Tooonug scooted back from the bushes and got to their feet. Tooonug angled away and out of sight from the castle to cut a path through the trees and underbrush. Stryker followed silently as best he could. After several minutes of traveling on a wide, curved bearing, Tooonug dropped to one knee. Stryker knelt next to him. Tooonug leaned forward onto his belly and started crawling. Stryker trailed, his face closely behind the moccasins.

Tooonug crawled behind another thicket of berry bushes and motioned for Stryker to move beside him. Tooonug then inched closer to the bushes and used a hand to carefully spread the branches. Stryker edged up next to him.

They were now viewing the castle's left rear corner. They saw a regular-sized door, iron reinforced, and very sturdy, built with heavy wood. Stryker figured the lock wouldn't be easy to open. From what he could see, he figured it unlatched from the inside.

"Let's move around to the other side," Stryker whispered. They did and found no other entrances. As Tooonug and Stryker lay prone on the ground, studying the walls, the Paiute nudged Stryker and gave a quick, short lift of his head toward the castle.

Stryker looked higher on the castle and saw a man walking along the wall walk. A lookout guard, he carried a rifle resting in the crook of an arm. *This is not going to be easy*, Stryker thought.

"We need a wagon," Stryker said when they'd returned to the horses. Tooonug nodded. Doubtful he understood what was on Stryker's mind. It didn't matter. He trusted the mixed breed knew what to do. He gave the Winchester back to Stryker and put the top hat back on.

Stryker and Tooonug rode to St Helena, a five-mile trip. It was a good road. Shadows getting longer off the buildings meant not much daylight left. Stryker reined the roan to stop in front of the two-story *St Helena General Store*. They dismounted and went inside.

"The folks in the castle, what do they usually buy?" Stryker asked the white-haired clerk wearing a cotton twill apron standing behind the counter.

"You ain't the regular man. What happened to Reeves?"

"Mister Sordid sent us."

"Supplies, tools, coffee, cheese, goods, tin goods, and just about anything else. You buying for 'em and forgot what you came for?"

"You're an intuitive man," Stryker said, forcing a grin. "Our wagon broke an axle right outside the castle." Stryker picked up on the presumption and went with it. "Reeves busted his ankle when the wagon tipped over." The shit got deeper. "We tried to fix it, but it started getting late, so we took the horses. Rode hard to get here and damn, I forgot what mister Sordid sent us to get. He's having some kind of shindig tonight and if I don't—"

"Don't worry, son. I know what he'll want. You'll need to borrow a wagon to haul it. Now you be sure and tell mister Sordid, Chester here is taking good care of him, won't ya?"

"I sure will."

"Colby," Chester called out to a youngster sweeping the floor. "Bring the buckboard 'round front here for mister… what did you say your name was?"

"Stryker." He figured ole Chester here was eager to make a killing on Sordid. "You think Gunther might want drink too?"

"Oh my gosh," Chester exclaimed. "Wine, he'll want plenty of that!" Chester feverishly raced his pencil across the paper pad. He penciled in *wine* and underlined it.

Guess they really don't make wine at the castle, mused Stryker. He watched as Chester completed a long list. Then, the enterprising entrepreneur hurried around the store, picking out choices of produce and vegetables, butter jars, bread loaves, cans of pears, peaches, and apples, a burlap sack of potatoes, paper sacks of flour and sugar, beans, cured hams, marinated cut beef in wired burlap, eggs, and more items Stryker didn't see get bagged. He put the meats in an iced crate. Then, of course, a good number of bottled wines, whites mostly, and a few reds. Chester had just about finished the selections when Colby came in the door.

"Horse and wagon's out front, mister Welby," Colby announced cheerfully.

"Good, load this stuff up while I figure out the bill." Chester dashed behind the counter and penciled out healthy dollar totals on the paper pad. When finished, he tore off two sheets and handed them to Stryker. "Tell mister Sordid I put it on his account, will you?" He put out his hand. "Pleasure doing business with you, Stryker."

Stryker accepted the offered handshake. It was no time to be rude. He pulled Tooonug by his tunic sleeve to rush outside.

They hitched the horses behind the wagon. Stryker pulled the carbine, handed it to Tooonug, and they climbed up to sit on the buck-board. Stryker made a clicking sound and snapped the reins.

"We get plenty food," Tooonug allowed as they drove out of town.

"Get ready." Those were the last words spoken as the two men rode to the castle. Both knew if they managed to get inside, there was a chance the two of them and Morgan would not make it out of the castle. Not alive, anyway. No need to discuss it. However, they had faced long odds before, and there was one thing in their favor—not many men were as proficient with gun and blade as the mixed breed and Tooonug.

It was fully dark by the time they arrived at the massive castle. Drawing closer, the stone monstrosity looked even more imposing against the night sky. "Stay in the wagon," Stryker hissed, and he hopped to the ground. He walked up to the iron-reinforced, ten-foot doors, and rapped the door knocker twice. He waited a few seconds. When no one answered, he banged louder.

"What you want?" A man on the parapet above him yelled.

Stryker stepped back from the doors to see where the voice came from. "Delivery for Gunther Sordid."

"Mister Sordid hasn't told me to expect a delivery."

"Chester at the general store in St Helena said it was a rush order." Stryker had used two names now. Might carry some weight.

"What's in the wagon?"

"Provisions for the party, a shindig Chester said. Lots of food and drink—wine and whiskey."

"Don't have any guests here tonight."

"Look, chum. Maybe it's a surprise party for you people, all the employees an' such." Stryker's thinking fast now. He played his last hole card. "Don't make no difference to me. I can turn around and take all this shit back."

"Hold on. I'll open the doors."

Stryker climbed back on the buckboard.

"You some talker," Tooonug deadpanned.

A minute later, the huge doors cranked open. Stryker drove the wagon under the stone archway and into the bailey yard. The courtyard was approximately a hundred feet deep and eighty feet wide. Wall sconces with kerosene lamps lit the interior castle every ten feet. On the left, were stables and a well pump. A tunnel corridor with open doorways about every fifteen feet ran along the right side. High above on the curtain walls, guards patrolled a wall walk. Stone steps at the four corners led to the wall walk.

Stryker counted two guards on the left wall and one on the other walkway looking down on him and Tooonug. They carried rifles. Two shorter sets of stone steps at the far end of the bailey yard led up to the great hall. Two men in the courtyard with guns approached the wagon. One was thin and tall with sloping shoulders, the other man just as tall and stouter. They wore dark suits, white shirts, and ties. In the flickering torch light, it was difficult for Stryker to clearly see them.

"Where's the kitchen?" Stryker shouted. "We got a wagon full of food and drink for the employee shindig."

"Whaaaat?" The taller one stuttered.

"Yeah, we got orders to deliver all this to the kitchen."

"Mister Sordid said nothing about it to me. Go ask him, Jorge," the stout guard ordered. Jorge spun and scurried up the steps to the great hall.

Shit. Stryker debated whether to start shooting or wait for Jorge to return. If the shooting started, they might not make it up the steps. The three guns on the wallwalk would have clear shots, and even in the dim light, the odds of making it up the steps weren't good. Tunnel doors were closer.

Stryker half-turned as if to look in the wagon. When he came back around, he held the Colt. He fired and the bullet struck the hefty guard in the chest, left center.

"The tunnel!" Stryker hissed to Tooonug. They leaped from the buckboard and dashed to the tunnel door. Shots were fired from above. Angry bullets whizzed around them as they ran. Tooonug, who was seated closer to the tunnel, got to the door first with Stryker close behind.

The narrow tunnel was torch-lit as well. "That way," Stryker yelled, pointing the Colt toward a set of stone steps on their left.

They sprinted up the steps to a heavy wooden door. It opened to another tunnel, a narrower stone corridor. Stryker shut the door behind them and slammed the bolt. The passageway was roughly three feet wide and Stryker had to stoop to keep from hitting his head on the rock ceiling. The walls and walkway were damp with moisture. Dank water glistened in the lamplight. Moving quickly down the slippery stones in the tunnel, they saw two more wood doors, both closed. One was located just ahead along the left wall and the other door stood at the tunnel's end. Stryker opened the first door. It led to the north end of the great hall. Stryker managed to see a long table surrounded by high-backed chairs and a door back of the big room before a swarm of bullets made him close the door. He flattened his back against the wall. Tooonug stood next to him.

"C'mon, Tooonug!" Stryker yelled.

Shouts behind them in the tunnel, sounded as if the guards had broken through the door. Tooonug turned and began firing the Winchester, throwing lead down the corridor. A man yelped in pain, then another one did as the bullets found flesh. Additional curses and shouts meant more guards and they returned Tooonug's fire.

Stryker ran to the last door, Tooonug right behind him, pumping the Winchester. Stryker got the small, but heavy door, open. He grabbed Tooonug by the collar and jerked the Paiute in behind him. Bullets thudded the wooden door after Stryker slammed it and slid the bolt shut.

They had come to a bedroom. Stryker spun around, his eyes quickly swept the room… there was Morgan.

She knelt on a large brass bed with arms extended, wrists shackled, and chained to iron rings anchored in the stone wall. Morgan wore a white shirt. It was a man's shirt that was far too big and half-unbuttoned. Her head drooped and a mess of hair covered her face. She didn't look up.

Stryker would have paid Morgan closer attention and ascertained if she lived, but she was not alone. Gunther Sordid with two armed guards stood on his left. Easy to recognize, the ancient Sordid wore a purple silk robe. He had a face only a grandmother could love. He might have been in his fifties. It was hard to tell. His sloping forehead, mushroom nose, and bulbous cheeks accented his small eyes. Fat lips partially hid bad teeth. A crown of black hair circled the bald dome. Though he wasn't overly obese, he carried two hundred pounds on a five-foot-six frame. *It would take a lot of cash or a lot of force for a woman to fuck him.*

They stood in an open doorway, peering out into the great hall, listening to the shooting. They whirled to Stryker and Tooonug when the door slammed.

Tooonug and Stryker fired at the same time. Both shots hit the same man. They fired a second volley and killed the second guard.

Gunther lifted his arms in surrender. The loose sleeves slid down his meaty arms to his biceps, or where they were supposed to be. "Don't shoot me," he wailed.

"Take him. Put a gun to his head," Stryker growled. He fought hard against killing Sordid outright. Knowing Tooonug would take longer to do it stopped him.

Tooonug wrapped an arm around Sordid's neck and kicked the door shut. He placed the carbine's barrel end at the base of Gunther's skull.

Stryker ran to the bed.

"Morgan," Stryker calmly said her name.

She struggled to lift her head. *She's alive.*

She was pathetically thin and emaciated. Her face was gaunt and hollow. Sharp bones protruded from a bare shoulder. Her naked thighs looked thin as well.

Stryker gently lifted Morgan's chin. "What happened here?" Anger boiled inside him.

"Thought you weren't com… starved my…." She went limp.

"Where's the key?" Stryker yelled at Sordid.

"In my pocket." Gunther dropped an arm and withdrew a brass key on a ring. He held it out, and Tooonug grabbed the ring and tossed it to Stryker.

Before Stryker could unlock the shackles, the door from the great hall burst open.

Five guards crowded into the chamber. The obvious leader, a short Mexican, maybe five-foot-four tall, hatless, and well-dressed in a black suit with a bolo tie, lowered his pistol. In a Latino accent, he gave the order for the rest of the men to do the same.

These men were different from the other guards.

The leader saw Morgan sitting on the bed. "Who is she?"

"My wife," Gunther said. He regained a bit of confidence. Five against two now.

"Why she chained?"

"That's my business. I hired you yesterday to protect me–Uunhh!" Tooonug tightened the hold around Gunther's neck.

"No, I'm not," Morgan groaned. Her head dropped again.

Stryker inserted the key in one of the cuffs.

The leader studied Stryker for a long moment, then Tooonug. "We go. He started for the door. His men turned to follow.

"Wait! Come back here, Tuco! I… Ugh"

Tooonug tightened his arm around Sordid's throat.

"She is not your woman," Tuco said. He and the rest of the Mexicans piled out the door.

Stryker finished freeing Morgan. He found her skirt on a chair in the corner and helped her put it on. When he lifted her from the bed, she felt pitifully light, not more than eighty-five pounds. He propped his leg on the bed and braced her back against his knee while he pulled the Peacemaker. Holding the gun under Morgan's body, he carried her across the room. Passing Tooonug, he said, "Not quick," and he continued out the door.

In the main hall, Stryker expected to see more guards. There were more, but to the mixed breed's surprise, they paid him no attention. Instead, the guards, a dozen or more, including the Mexicans, were busy unloading the wagon, bringing food and drink into the great hall, and placing it onto the enormous banquet table.

Tuco saw Stryker carrying Morgan down the stone stairs and approached him. "Woman *mucho* skinny, *Senior*. Give *Senorita* food?" Tuco waved his hand by his mouth as if he were eating.

Stryker had only thought of getting Morgan away from the place. However, he now realized she might die before he got her back to San Francisco. She needed food, especially liquids. A person can live weeks without food, but only about a week without water. "Yes. But only a little." Stryker was familiar with starvation victims. He had witnessed cases in Rebel prisons and knew to go slow with Morgan.

"Bread and water," Stryker said. "Get it from the kitchen. Sordid is dead." *Well, maybe not yet.*

"Arturo!" Tuco called to one of his men shouldering a sack of potatoes.

Arturo plopped the sack on the banquet table. "Que queires, Tuco?"

"Arturo, go to *cocina*. Bring crackers, bread, water *por la* Senorita. *Ve rapido!*" Tuco added crackers.

Heaving the potato sack onto the table, Arturo scurried to the kitchen.

Stryker placed Morgan in a chair by the enormous table. She slumped against an armrest. He was shocked at how frail she looked. Bones protruded all over, her face, arms, and legs, but it was her eyes that scared him. The orbs stared at him from dark recessed caverns. *She really tried to kill herself.*

He sat beside her. "You've got to eat before we head back," Stryker said with concern written on his face.

Morgan nodded weakly.

Arturo hurried from the kitchen door, carrying the wheat items and more in a checkered napkin. He held a mug of water under the napkin. "I bring boiled egg and chicken *tambien*," Arturo said proudly. He set the water and food on the table.

Morgan tried to pick at it and Stryker let her take her time eating. He gripped her shoulder and braced her back with the other hand. She drank some of the water and took a bite of each piece of food, including the fried chicken breast. It took twenty minutes. "I don't think I can eat more," she finally whispered and sat back from the table.

Tuco had been sitting across from Morgan sipping whiskey. He nodded to Stryker, "She *is* your woman."

Stryker bent to pick up Morgan and saw Tooonug come from the bedroom with a wool blanket. He and Stryker carefully wrapped it around her. *Thanks, Tooonug.*

"Let's go." Stryker gathered Morgan in his arms and started for the wagon. Tooonug followed and helped lift her in. The Paiute drove the wagon to St Helena. Stryker sat in the back holding Morgan and she fell asleep. Even though she was skin and bones, it felt good to hold her. Caressing her shoulder, he watched the roan and gelding trailing behind.

Although emaciated, Morgan was still attractive to Stryker. Her determination drew him to her, even if she was trying to take her own life. Had he not found Morgan tonight, he believed she would have died in a day or two. He nudged her closer. She moaned quietly in her sleep. *God, you feel good.* He watched the horses' bobbing heads and thought about how much he cared for the woman beside him.

A sordid death.

Gunther woke from being unconscientious by Tooonug who had knocked him out with the barrel of the Winchester. Still dizzy, his head throbbing in pain, he tried to rub his forehead. He couldn't reach his face. His other arm wouldn't reach either. Sordid's arms were shackled. He was naked on the bed and chained to the wall like he'd shackled Morgan. He felt cold. A white sheet covered his lower body. He searched for his clothes and didn't see them.

Something hung from the brass footrail. He squinted to make out what it was. It was difficult to see clearly in the flickering lantern light. Looks like sausages. A puzzled look and anger crossed his face. *Food? What the hell? They gonna starve me while I look at it? The fucking bastards!* He screamed out, "Guards, get in here!"

Gunther studied the meat. It dripped. He tried to sit up and lean forward to get a closer look, but it hurt. It hurt bad. He felt intense pain in his abdomen. He looked down and saw the expanding dark stain on the sheet. He then realized, those were not sausages on the footrail. Gunther Sordid, the quixotic Marxist and certifiable asshole, died before sunrise.

Tooonug drove the wagon up to the railroad station at fifteen past ten. "No more trains tonight. Next train west was the nine ten in the morning," the ticket agent groused and he closed the window.

Stryker climbed onto the buckboard with Tooonug, leaving the sleeping Morgan in the back, and drove the wagon down Main Street. Coal-gasified street lamps provided lighting in the town of eighteen-hundred and three houses down from the station, they came to a painted sign. "Room and Board," Tooonug stayed with Morgan in the wagon while Stryker went inside. He woke up a haggard-looking woman on the first floor and paid her four dollars for two rooms. Stryker went back out to the wagon. They took it behind the house to the run-in shed, where they unhitched the draft horse. After putting halters on all three horses and giving them food and water, Stryker woke Morgan. They entered the rear door of the house and Stryker helped Morgan climb stairs to the second floor. He unlocked the door to room *three* and handed the key to room four to Tooonug. Sleep for two of the guests came easy. Stryker lay awake next to Morgan, and he finally drifted off several hours later.

The next morning after breakfast, they loaded in the wagon and rode to the station. Although only a short distance, Morgan remained too weak to walk. She did eat a bowl of oatmeal and told Stryker she felt better. She rested next to Tooonug on a bench while Stryker bought fare for them and the two horses to Vallejo. Tooonug then drove the wagon to the general store, parked it out front, and trotted back to the station.

Five other people waited in the station as well. None of them seemed to know one another and no one talked. A folded newspaper next to Tooonug remained untouched. Tooonug couldn't read and Stryker didn't ask him for it. It was not good to embarrass a man who helped rescue Morgan. Stryker's attention was on Morgan anyway. So, he wrapped an arm around her thin shoulders and waited for the train.

Finally, a distant train whistle blew. Morgan sat up, looking at the tracks through the open door. Stryker noticed her staring and wondered if she was eager for the train to get her away from this place. She was.

They arrived in Vallejo a few minutes before noon after making scheduled, but frustrating, stops along the way. Stryker turned in the gelding and the three of them, with the roan, boarded the ferry to San Francisco at two-fifteen. Morgan dozed most of the trip, resting her head against Stryker's shoulder. He sat quietly and still so he didn't disturb her. The ferry was only half full and they were able to sit by themselves. Tooonug remained his usual stoic self, staring straight ahead with who-knows-what, occupying his mind.

Stryker took Tooonug out of San Francisco to The Stratford Horse

Farm and bought him three very fine palominos. He bought train tickets for Tooonug and his horses to Salt Lake City and gave the Paiute five hundred dollars in gold coins. At the station, they placed a hand on one another's shoulders, instead of shaking hands, and then parted without speaking. So then, Stryker *does* have one friend, a very good friend. Tooonug.

Since Morgan's kidnapping, the days were made longer with worry. What Sordid had attempted to do with socialist ransom demands was bigger than Morgan. Stryker knew that, but his focus had been on her. Now that she sat safely beside him, he was free to contemplate what Sordid tried to do. Evil, that's how Stryker viewed socialism. He had seen its workings up close in Egalitaria; socialism confiscated a man's wealth. Even worse, it robbed him of his soul. Marxist leaders pontificate scathingly of greedy capitalists, but it is the dictatorial leaders of collectivism ensconced in their expensive mansions, who are greedy. How so many people didn't see that puzzled Stryker.

It took several weeks before Morgan seemed to recover mentally. Even so, Stryker caught her occasionally looking furtively around corners. He began to doubt if the fear of another kidnapping would ever leave her.

After three weeks in San Francisco, Morgan reached for him in bed. Stryker had not asked for sex, assuming she needed time. He learned Sordid had raped her repeatedly and that was why she tried to starve herself to death. She apologized to Stryker for not putting up more of a fight. She had felt guilty about it. He told her how Sordid died but that brought her no satisfaction. Morgan did not know why Sordid kidnapped her. She thought it was for sex. Stryker gave the real purpose. Her face darkened when she found out. Morgan had seen her town, Bickford, become Egalitaria. Marxist thugs killed her husband and took everything they owned. Her hatred of socialism ran deeper than Stryker's.

Morgan's unwarranted guilt was assuaged somewhat when Stryker informed her, he had made two such *sacrifices* during his quest to find her. She should not feel bad. He informed her he was no saint. Morgan smiled pensively when he told her during dinner. That night she reached for him in bed.

"I want you."

Stryker rolled on his side facing Morgan. Propping his head on bent elbow, he reached over and swept a few stray hairs from her forehead, then leaned down and brushed his lips against her brow.

Morgan lay with closed eyes and Stryker ran fingertips lightly around her breasts. He dragged the backs of his fingers around the soft skin and gently squeezed her nipples. Leaning closer, he blew on a nipple and flicked it with his tongue. The nipples firmed and he massaged the little nubs between thumb and forefinger. As he continued to play with her breasts, Stryker placed little kisses on Morgan's face, on her eyes, her cheeks, and finally, on her lips, where she returned his kiss.

He moved his mouth near Morgan's ear and whispered an endearment, that would be unspoken except between the two of them. She twitched her lips into a smile and whispered, "Me too."

Stryker leaned back and delicately dragged his fingers down Morgan's body to tussle short hair down there. Morgan spread her thighs. Touching the velvet areas inside her upper thighs, he allowed his fingers to linger, enjoying the feel of her skin. When he gently ran a finger up her vagina, she felt wet. He brought his hand to his mouth before returning it to leisurely twirl around a swollen clitoris.

"You like?" he whispered.

"Yes." Morgan spread her thighs a little wider. He teased her, barely stroking her lips until Morgan grabbed his hand and held it against her.

She was very wet now, ready, and eager. Stryker swung on top and started slowly. He fought hard against the urge to get on with it, but that was not tonight. He withdrew, not all the way, just enough to make room for Morgan's hand he placed on her clitoris. He held it there, making her move her hand on herself. He learned long ago only a woman knows how to caress the sensitive little nub, time an orgasm, drawing it out for maximum pleasure. Morgan masturbated as he moved slowly in and out. She had multiple elongated orgasms. He didn't count. He let her rest a while and began again. She had more, but when she had to work for the last one, he pumped faster and came. He paused, started over, working harder, and he came again. Morgan joined him with one of her own.

There was nothing extraordinary, no wild exotic play, no heroics. Not after what she'd been through. Stryker rightly figured Morgan just wanted lovemaking, comfort food.

Afterward, they lay next to each other. He circled an arm under Morgan's neck and caressed her hair until she fell asleep.

NOTES

CHAPTER 2

i. , Trouble in Tahoe: Book VI in the Evil Stryker Series

CHAPTER 5

i. Ladies of the Evening Marker; https://www.atlasobscura.com/places/ladies-of-the-evening-historical-marker
ii. Cross Cut: Book II in the Evil Stryker Series

CHAPTER 7

i. , [vi] Art of the Kill: Book VII in the Evil Stryker Series

CHAPTER 9

i. Left to Die: Book I in the Evil Stryker Series

ACKNOWLEDGMENTS

Thanks to my dear wife, Pamela Mitchell, and my indispensable editor, Stacey Smekofske.

ABOUT WES RAND

Wes Rand was an Artillery Officer in the U.S. Army during the 1960s. He pays alimony. He doesn't like to golf but lives on a golf course. He has been bucked off a horse and two women.

He has a cabin in the mountains where he writes and hikes while his wife plays golf in Las Vegas. Wes enjoys living under the open skies in Nevada and Utah.

Follow Evil Stryker and Wes Rand at EvilStryker.com

facebook.com/wes.rand.14

instagram.com/rand.wes

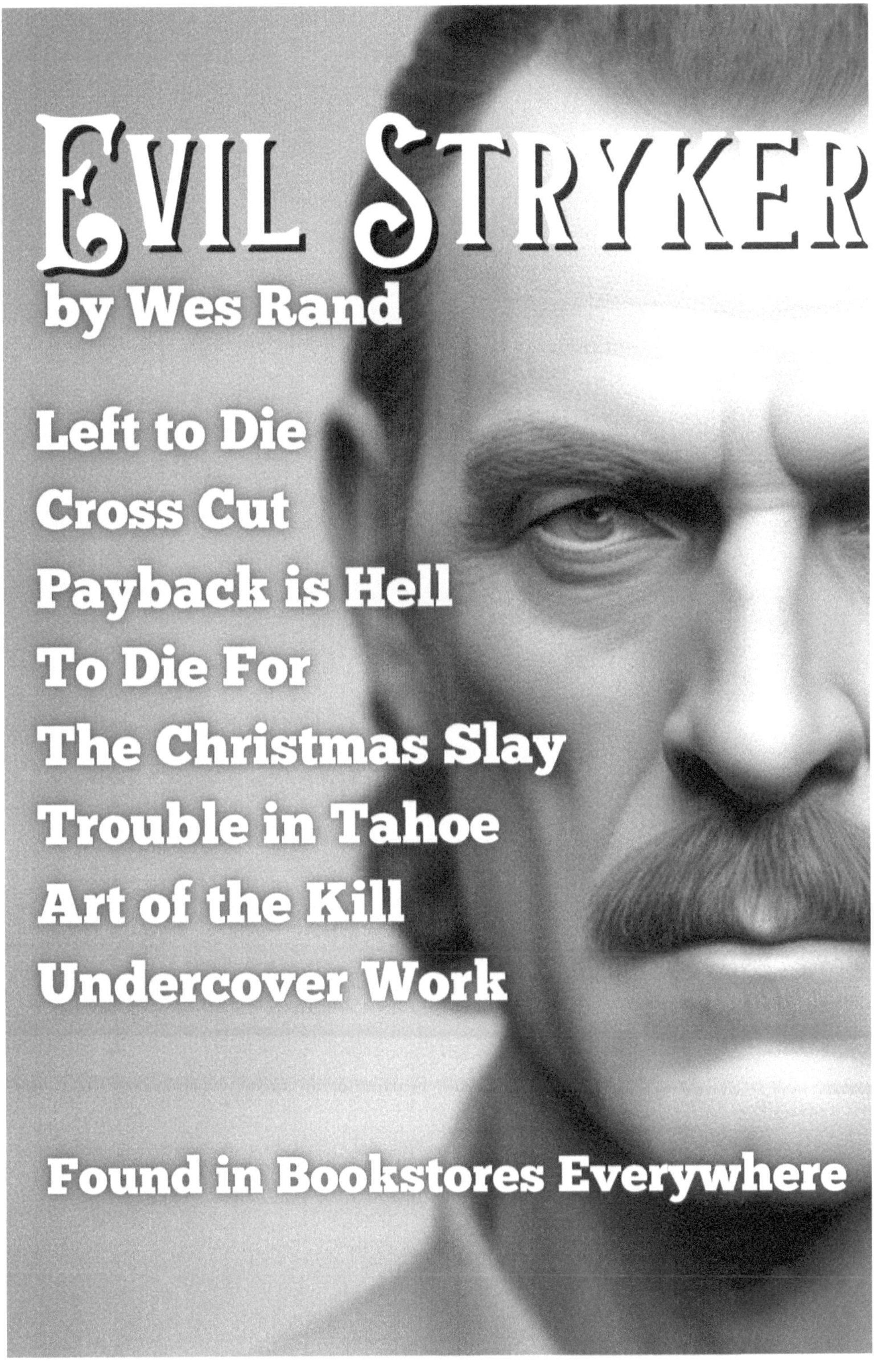

Evil Stryker

by Wes Rand

Left to Die

Cross Cut

Payback is Hell

To Die For

The Christmas Slay

Trouble in Tahoe

Art of the Kill

Undercover Work

Found in Bookstores Everywhere